"I don't ___ ___ ___ impression, here ...

"but you're much more valuable to me as a nanny, someone to love and to care for my children, than you are for ... for ... Well, than you are in any other capacity. So what do you say we sort of draw up some kind of truce?"

"A truce?" Perry asked, remembering the kiss they'd shared.

"Well," Mike said, then swallowed as if what he had to say was difficult. "Not really a truce, just a pact to keep things impersonal between us."

Perry started to laugh. "We have to make a pact to keep things impersonal? Can't we just admit we find each other attractive and forget it? Can't we go on the honor system?"

"Apparently not," Mike said. Then he sighed and gave her a look that sent her pulse racing. "We seem to have some sort of wild chemistry, Perry, and I *will* admit that I'm having a heck of a time controlling it...."

Dear Reader,

Welcome to the fourth great month of CELEBRATION 1000! We're winding up this special event with fireworks!—six more dazzling love stories that will light up your summer nights. The festivities begin with *Impromptu Bride* by beloved author Annette Broadrick. While running for their lives, Graham Douglas and Katie Kincaid had to marry. But will their hasty wedding lead to everlasting love?

Favorite author Elizabeth August will keep you enthralled with *The Forgotten Husband*. Amnesia keeps Eloise from knowing the real reason she'd married rugged, brooding Jonah Tavish. But brief memories of sweet passion keep her searching for the truth.

This month our FABULOUS FATHER is *Daniel's Daddy*—a heartwarming story by Stella Bagwell.

Debut author Kate Thomas brings us a tale of courtship—Texas-style in—*The Texas Touch*.

There's love and laughter when a runaway heiress plays *Stand-in Mom* in Susan Meier's romantic romp. And don't miss Jodi O'Donnell's emotional story of a love all but forgotten in *A Man To Remember*.

We'd love to know if you have enjoyed CELEBRATION 1000! Please write to us at the address shown below.

Happy reading!

Anne Canadeo
Senior Editor

Please address questions and book requests to:
Silhouette Reader Service
U.S.: 3010 Walden Ave., P.O. Box 1325, Buffalo, NY 14269
Canadian: P.O. Box 609, Fort Erie, Ont. L2A 5X3

STAND-IN MOM
Susan Meier

Silhouette
ROMANCE™
Published by Silhouette Books
America's Publisher of Contemporary Romance

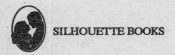

SILHOUETTE BOOKS

RECYCLED PAPER · RECYCLED PAPER

ISBN 0-373-19022-0

STAND-IN MOM

Copyright © 1994 by Linda Susan Meier

This edition published by arrangement with Harlequin Enterprises B.V.

® and TM are trademarks of Harlequin Enterprises B.V., used under license. Trademarks indicated with ® are registered in the United States Patent and Trademark Office, the Canadian Trade Marks Office and in other countries.

Printed in U.S.A.

SUSAN MEIER

is a wife, mother and romance writer. She firmly believes that, in romance, sometimes it's not what you say but how you say it. Therefore, the most simple events can be made to sound beautiful.

When she's not writing or working, she's probably watching movies—which she counts as one of her greatest interests—or reading.

MOMY WANTED: TALL, PRETY, SOFT,

CAN BAKE COOKIES AND CARRY

A BEAR IN HER TEETH. AND WILL

~~LIKE~~ LOVE MY DADDY

AND 2 BROTHERS. AND

ME.

Prologue

"It looks like Arthur's at it again."

Perry Pierson rose from her tall-backed beige leather chair and paced to the wall of windows behind her desk. Cora, Perry's former nanny who now worked as her assistant, sat still and silent, watching Perry as she brought her hands to her face, then tapped her index fingers against her pursed lips.

"We can't let him get away with this," Perry said, turning from the windows to face Cora. The light from a brass floor lamp surrounded Perry, dancing through her strawberry-blond hair like fairy dust. Her simple peach wool suit spoke eloquently of Perry's wealth, even as her delicate features, trim figure and natural grace complemented it.

"No, we can't," Cora agreed. "And we can't go to your father. He thinks the sun rises and sets on Arthur. Without substantial proof, he'd never believe his right-hand man was trying to run small newspapers out of business. Arthur's slick. Unless you can think of a plan, you're not going to stop him."

"Okay, we don't really have proof that Arthur's doing anything," Perry said. "All we know is that Arthur's made several trips to Ebensburg and now Mike McGuire's newspaper is losing employees. We can't confront Arthur because he'll only promise to stop and then sneak into Ebensburg, with the power of my father's name and the backing of my father's money. He would eventually wear Mike McGuire down until he closes his paper and agrees to go to work for Arthur."

She leaned back on her chair and tapped her index fingers against her lips again. "So, the only other option available is to somehow warn Mike McGuire, and give him the help he needs to fight Arthur."

"Are you nuts?" Cora said incredulously. "What if you call him and he doesn't believe you? Worse, what if you lay out a plan for him and he turns around and contacts your father? Your father would be absolutely furious that you dragged an outsider into a problem that should have remained in the company."

"Okay, you're right," Perry agreed as she reached out and grasped the private investigator's file, which had been delivered earlier that evening, pulled it from her desk and opened the folder. "It says here that McGuire has already lost two of his advertising salespeople and one reporter." She glanced up and looked Cora in the eye. "I don't think it would take a whole heck of a lot to convince him that his operation's being sabotaged."

"I'm not saying that. What I'm saying is that we don't know how he'd react to the news, so before we can take him into our confidence, we have to be sure he'll be receptive to working with us. We should send somebody down there to infiltrate Mike McGuire's office by taking one of those jobs that are now open. Somebody who could spend a little time figuring out what kind of guy Mike McGuire is before we tell him what we suspect.''

''No, we've got to keep it down to just you and me. We can't risk getting anyone else involved in this. One of *us* is going to have to... wait a minute.''

''What?''

''It says here that he has even lost his baby-sitter, housekeeper. This is ridiculous!''

''I sincerely doubt that Arthur paid off Mike McGuire's nanny.''

''He would if he knew Mike McGuire was a divorced man with custody of his three kids,'' Perry said. ''Arthur doesn't stop at anything. Not only is he sabotaging Mike McGuire's business, but getting rid of Mike McGuire's housekeeper almost assures that the poor man is tipped off balance by the problems at home, so that the next time Arthur makes an offer, McGuire might just be desperate enough to take it.''

''That does make a weird kind of sense.''

''You're darn right it does!'' Perry said vehemently. ''I can't just sit back and let Arthur ruin this man's whole life. I've got to do something.''

''Like what?'' Cora asked.

''I'm not exactly sure, but I'll have plenty of time to figure it out on the drive down to Ebensburg tonight.''

''Drive? Perry! Ebensburg's in Pennsylvania! That's got to be at least nine hours from Boston.''

''I know, but I don't want either of the company pilots inadvertently telling Arthur that they took me there,'' Perry said, rising from her chair. ''That would look a little obvious, don't you think?''

''Perry, you need to think this through. Take a day or two—''

''No. Every day we wait adds to Arthur's advantage.''

"Perry, please, just remember that if your dad finds out, he's going to go through the roof, and don't do anything—"

"He won't find out until I have the proof I need."

"And how do you plan on keeping Mike McGuire from telling him?"

"Cora, you're forgetting that this is a desperate man. He is not going to bite a hand that's offering to feed him."

"Yeah, well, you just be careful."

Perry began to laugh. "I'm twenty-eight now, Cora, and I've matured since I started to work here. I'm not going to burst into Mike McGuire's office and act like his guardian angel. I'll meet him at his house and gain his confidence and his trust before I tell him anything."

"Just don't get too cocky. You know what they say about the best laid plans of mice and men."

"You're such a pessimist! I'm going down there to help this man, not hurt him! What could possibly go wrong?"

Chapter One

Perry Pierson stared at the tall, incredibly handsome man who held open the weather-beaten farmhouse door, and completely forgot the introductory speech she'd labored to compose on the long drive from Boston to Ebensburg, Pennsylvania.

Mike McGuire's thick black hair shone like a well-cut onyx ring, and even though he'd obviously just shaved, his face was very sexily shaded by a shadowy beard on his well-defined cheeks, jaw and chin. His eyes were as blue as the sky of a lazy August afternoon, but their gaze was direct, razor sharp, very penetrating, very potent. His full lips were twisted into something akin to a half frown, half sneer.

She hadn't expected a warm reception once he discovered her identity, but she hadn't even introduced herself yet and already he was scowling.

"All right, come in," he said, jerking the wooden door to give her a wider berth. As he pulled back the door, she stepped inside his home, trying to adjust her eyes as she came in out of the bright autumn sunshine. The entrance hall of the farmhouse was dark, but that was caused by furnishings and decor, not design. The little foyer was full of treasures, an ornate chandelier and thick brown wood-work—both of which were overshadowed by heavy red velvet wallpaper.

"I'm not exactly thrilled by your arrival," her host announced, and, remembering her mission, Perry spun around to face him, then almost regretted she had. Not only did he look big, he looked angry. Incredibly angry. Standing in front of the door, shrouded by the only beam of sunlight penetrating the entranceway through a small, uncurtained window, with his white shirtsleeves rolled to his elbows as if he were about to get into a fistfight, not begin the day's work, Mike McGuire continued with his piercing gaze.

Of all the possible scenarios and reactions she and Cora had considered, they'd never once thought Mike McGuire would find out she was on her way, but obviously he had. Not only did that mean Arthur Tyrone had somehow gotten wind of her plan, but he'd sabotaged her by warning Mike McGuire. Still, she and Cora had been so careful, Perry couldn't believe that had happened and her voice was full of doubt when she said, "You were expecting me?"

"At seven a.m.," he replied sarcastically, then glanced at his watch for emphasis.

Perry cocked her head in confusion. Even in their best estimate, she and Cora hadn't thought she'd arrive that early. In fact, she'd been afraid he would have already gone to work before she could get to his house. "Seven?" she asked, totally confused, but also very curious. "Why seven?"

"Hey, let's not play games here. I know I told my mother to tell you to be here at seven."

"Your mother..."

"Look, just because I've been searching for a house-keeper for almost a month, doesn't mean I'm so desperate I'll tolerate your being late. My mother might have hired you, but whether you like it or not, you still have to prove yourself to me. And that means you arrive on time. The children's nanny must be here by seven."

Despite the fact that she'd driven through the night to get to Ebensburg and, therefore, hadn't slept in over twenty-four hours, Perry had read the private investigator's report so many times that she instantly remembered Mike Mc-Guire needed a housekeeper and it looked as if his mother had hired one for him. He wasn't expecting Perry, or any representative of Omnipotence. He thought Perry was his new housekeeper. Relief flooded through her.

"Oh, I'm sorry," she quickly apologized. "I think you have the wrong impression here...."

"I don't think I do," he disagreed, again piercing her with a killer stare, before he turned, grabbed his briefcase and then began walking toward the stairway, moving briskly, like a man on an unexpectedly tight schedule.

"Wait a minute," Perry said, scampering after him. She grabbed his elbow and urged him to face her. "You've made a mistake. You see, I'm—"

"Save it for somebody else. I don't take very well to excuses. Right now, you've got two things going for you. Number one, my mother hired you, so you must be a very good person because Mary McGuire wouldn't trust her grandkids to just anybody. And number two, I might not be desperate yet, but I am in a jam. So do yourself a favor and don't spoil things by giving me some half-baked reason for being late to work on your first day."

"But I'm—"

He pressed his index finger to her lips to silence her and little pin prickles of electricity radiated from his skin through her lips, and down to her toes. "Let me give you an important piece of advice. When you're late for this job, you make me late for my job, which means your biggest responsibility is to get here on time. If you can't do that, then I'll have to find somebody else. So don't push me.''

They were nearly nose to nose, and this close, his bright blue eyes seemed to give off sparks. Without warning, a river of indescribable, incomprehensible feelings flowed through Perry. His nearness was overpowering, though not in a frightening way, and not even as the challenge he may have wished to inspire—unless fear felt hot and cold, and a challenge had a shivery tingle to it. And Perry knew they didn't.

Realizing she had more important concerns than the strange, unfamiliar sensations coursing through her, Perry blinked up at Mike McGuire. She'd never in her entire life met anybody like him, because never in her entire life would anyone dare speak in this tone or this way to Graham Pierson's daughter. This man was going to be more than a little bit embarrassed when he realized he wasn't just reprimanding the wrong person, he was harassing the woman who held his future in her hands.

Remembering her purpose, she found her best professional voice. ''Mr. McGuire. I—''

''Uh-uh-uh,'' he said, stepping away from her. ''We don't want to spoil our relationship at this early stage. Excuses only irritate me, remember?''

Perry smiled sarcastically. ''Oh, I'm sure I'll remember.''

''Good, I'm glad we understand each other.''

With that, he walked to the door, reached for his suit jacket, which was hanging on the banister of a long wooden stairway off to the right, hung it over his arm, then bounded out the door. But he stopped abruptly and turned to face her. ''The twins caught the bus at seven-thirty, but you'll have Mitzie all day. Then you'll have the boys again at three-thirty when they get home from school. I won't be back until around six."

He turned again, pulled the door closed, and the next sound Perry heard was the thump, thump, thump of his footfalls as they pounded on the wide steps of his plank porch.

She could have stopped him. Actually, she knew she *should* have stopped him. But there was a part of her that wanted the satisfaction of strolling into his office later this morning with proof of identification and the plan to beat Arthur, which she'd created on the long ride down. She wanted to see Mike McGuire's chin hit his desk and then hear apologies roll off his tongue. In fact, she was downright looking forward to it.

She heard the car engine start, heard the sound of the vehicle as it began to move away, and smiled. It would be very interesting to hear how he justified leaving her with his child when she'd tried several times to explain she wasn't the new nanny. But more than that, it may prove beneficial to have him at an embarrassing disadvantage, particularly considering that even though she was here to help him, she also needed his help.

"Who are you?"

Startled out of her reverie, Perry turned to see the cutest kid in the world watching her from between the wooden pegs of the banister. Long straight locks of black hair dangled down the front of the child's candy-striped nightgown, and the bear the little girl was holding looked suspiciously like the bear in the picture embossed on the top of her nightie.

"I'm Perry. Who are you?"

"Mitzie," the little girl replied, easing her way down the steps. Her right hand clutched the thick wooden banister. Her ragged bear dangled over the crook of her elbow. "Are you the keeper?" she asked hopefully.

"Am I the what?" Perry asked, confused.

"The keeper," the little girl happily repeated. Walking down the wide steps seemed to be a real challenge for tiny Mitzie, and every time her feet thumped onto a new step, her black hair bobbed.

Perry smiled. She remembered when it was a major victory to climb the circular stairway of her father's foyer, and when looking up at the landing was as impossible as trying to look behind a cloud. "What's a keeper?"

"Mrs. Martin was a keeper. She did dishes. She made lunch."

"Oh, *house*keeper!" Perry said, finally understanding. "No. I'm not the keeper," she immediately denied. "But it looks like I might be taking care of you for a while."

"Dad can't find a keeper," Mitzie announced with ominous seriousness as she finished her descent. She stopped directly in front of Perry and looked down, but then her gaze traveled upward, slowly inspecting Perry from the tips of her bone leather pumps to the top of her strawberry-blond chignon. To see above Perry's waist, Mitzie arched her neck so far, Perry feared the child would tumble backward, so Perry reached down and lifted Mitzie into her arms to give the little girl a better view.

When they were face-to-face, Perry saw a lot more in Mitzie's expression than idle curiosity. This tiny child might be as light as a feather, but she was as serious as an owl, and Perry really couldn't blame her. It would be frightening for anyone to wake up and discover a stranger in their house. For a child, it was probably as close to terrifying as anything could come. For a moment Mitzie studied Perry and Perry said nothing, giving Mitzie the opportunity to get comfortable, while Perry took notice of a few things, herself.

Mitzie didn't have the face of a chubby cherub, but rather the well-defined features of a woman. Her deep-set blue eyes were the perfect complement to high cheekbones, a well-shaped mouth and a pert little nose. Even her long, straight hair had a thicker, more mature appearance than the usual feathery locks of a child.

Curious, Perry couldn't resist asking, "How old are you?"

The little girl grinned up at her. "Four."

"Four. That's a great age," Perry said, since Mitzie seemed to be so proud of it. Then she balanced Mitzie's bottom on the crook of her arm and smiled. "I guess your dad didn't tell you, but your grandmother found a keeper."

Mitzie still studied Perry's face with keen interest. "I think *you* should be the keeper. You should stay," Mitzie said, locking the gaze of her blue eyes with that of Perry's brown ones.

It was on the tip of Perry's tongue to tell this lovely little girl that it would be a cold frosty day in hell before Perry would work for Mitzie's dad in any capacity, and that the tables were about to turn and Mitzie's daddy would need to work with Perry if he wanted to save his company, but she stopped herself. This innocent child was too darned young and too darned cute to have a stranger spoil her illusions about her father.

"I can't," Perry answered, taking advantage of the simple truth as she smiled at the beautiful toddler in her arms. "Your dad already hired a housekeeper."

"Oh," Mitzie said, nodding with understanding, though she seemed a bit confused. She slid her arms around Perry's neck and sighed. "I wish you could stay."

The feeling of the soft skin of Mitzie's arms around Perry's neck did the strangest things to her nervous system, and the worst part of it was Perry couldn't identify what or why. She'd never held a child before. In fact, she rarely saw any. Her world was filled with pristine offices, lawyers and business managers, not beautiful little girls with pleading blue eyes who could almost make you bend to their wishes, even when to do so was impossible.

She cleared her throat. "Where are your slippers?" Perry asked, changing the subject. "Little girls aren't supposed to come downstairs unless they're wearing slippers."

"Did your mom tell you that?" Mitzie asked with a gasp.

"No," Perry admitted curiously, surprised both by Mitzie's reaction and the strange sincerity with which the question was asked. "When I was a little girl, I wasn't allowed out of my room unless I was fully dressed."

"Did your mom tell you *that?*" Mitzie asked in an excited voice that caused Perry to peer at her before she answered. Mitzie's blue eyes were wide and round with childish curiosity.

"No. My nanny did."

Deflated, Mitzie sighed. "You don't have a mom, either."

"My mother died when I was very young," Perry explained softly, watching Mitzie's puckered face. "But my dad hired a wonderful woman, Cora, to be my nanny, and she acted just like my mother."

"My mom left," Mitzie mumbled through lips that hardly moved.

"Oh," Perry said, then she swallowed. What kind of mother could leave a cute little girl like this?

"S'okay," Mitzie said, shrugging.

No, it was not okay, Perry wanted to disagree, but she stayed silent, thinking as she watched Mitzie's sad face. Even if Perry didn't know firsthand how lonely life could be for a little girl without a mother, Mitzie's expression would have told the story now, and Perry was struck with an odd but distinct feeling that fate could sometimes be very heartless. Not only had this poor child been deserted by her mother, but she'd been left with a seemingly insensitive, rather brusque father.

"Can I have oatmeal for breakfast?" Mitzie asked quietly, moving on to the next topic as though she'd been through this before and knew very well no grown-up had any answers for her.

"How about cold cereal this morning?" Perry hedged. The last thing in the world she wanted to do was deny this sweet child anything, but the truth of the matter was, her cooking experience went about as far as opening a box and pouring on milk.

"I like oatmeal," Mitzie said.

"I like oatmeal, too, but," Perry began, then she sighed. How in the world did anybody deny those blue eyes anything? "Look, kid, can you keep a secret?"

Eager to please, Mitzie nodded.

"I don't know how to make oatmeal. In fact, I can't cook at all."

"You can't?" Mitzie gasped. Her eyes grew round with surprise and Perry started to laugh.

"No, I can't, but I know somebody who can and I'm going to give her a call right now. So why don't you run upstairs and grab your slippers?"

"Are you going to stay?" Mitzie asked hopefully.

Perry blew her breath out on a long sigh. "I can't."

"Please," Mitzie pleaded in earnest. "I like you."

Unexpectedly, Perry thought of the man with hair as black as a moonless midnight and unsmiling blue eyes, and it tickled her funny bone to think of his reaction if she really did stay. Not only had she never cooked, but the closest thing to housekeeping she'd ever done was picking up her toys when she was six. If that man could be provoked into anger by a late employee, he'd probably explode the first time he tried to eat Perry's cooking. That is, if she didn't poison him.

"Mitzie, you know I will stay until your real baby-sitter gets here...."

"Please?"

"Mitzie, your dad hired someone," Perry said, unwilling to hurt this child by arguing with her, though she knew she had to be honest. "She's simply not here yet. So, why don't we just try to make the best of the time we have. Who knows? We may have a whole hour to play before your nanny gets here and that means the quicker you get your slippers, the quicker we can get to playing."

Seeming to understand that logic, Mitzie nodded furiously, then loosened her grip and slid down Perry's peach wool skirt to the floor.

Perry watched Mitzie as the child bounded up the stairs as carefree as a new bunny in a meadow, and, again, Perry was struck by a feeling she couldn't define or describe, except to admit that she didn't feel uncomfortable as she should have felt with a child. In fact, part of her felt strangely close to Mitzie, a result, Perry was sure, of the shared experience of their both being motherless.

Shaking her head at her meanderings, Perry turned and began to search for a phone. She walked through the dusty living room and into the next room, which was small, cramped with furniture and cluttered with so many papers, she almost didn't see the phone cord, which dangled down the side of the desk.

Seeking only to uncover the phone, Perry began moving correspondence, magazines and documents, but like a neon sign, the silver and gold letterhead of Omnipotence didn't merely catch her attention, it caused her to gasp. At the bottom of the very neatly printed letter was a familiar signature. Arthur Tyrone.

She spent the next few seconds convincing herself that she had no right to read this letter and got so caught up in trying to put it down unread that she didn't hear the sound of the back door opening, neither did she hear Mike McGuire approach. The first she knew he was standing in the doorway of the den, watching her, was when he very quietly, very calmly asked, "Looking for anything in particular?"

Chapter Two

For the first time in her life, Perry Pierson found herself absolutely speechless. She knew her mouth hung open guiltily, and the paper she was holding would condemn her, even though she'd done nothing wrong. For a whole thirty seconds, she merely stared at the man who stood before her waiting for an answer, until she realized he didn't look nearly as angry as he had when he'd left her fifteen minutes before. His full lips were drawn upward slightly, almost enough that Perry might consider them to be forming a smile.

Encouraged by that thought, she cleared her throat. "Actually, I was looking for the telephone."

"Well, you can use that one," he said, indicating the instrument she'd recently uncovered. "But there's a wall phone in the kitchen."

"Thanks," she said, then swallowed because she knew she wasn't completely out of the woods yet. Trying to look casual and calm, she turned and set the letter on his desk again, but before it was even halfway to its destination, Mike McGuire reached out and slid it from her fingers.

"I can understand why you were staring at this. It's interesting letterhead, isn't it?"

"Yes. It's beautiful."

"Beautiful?" he echoed sarcastically. "I think it's pretentious and arrogant. Omnipotence," he said, reading the company name as if it were a curse. "Not Omnipotence Publications. Oh, no. That would be too revealing. Just Omnipotence." Staring at the piece of correspondence as if it were a living, breathing thing, he shook his head, and Perry took two paces backward, unconsciously stepping away from him. "I'd love to get my hands on somebody from that company right now."

Taking yet another step away from him, Perry swallowed. His tone of voice was calm, making his words sound sensible and rational, but their meaning was very plain. And if that wasn't enough, the expression on his face very definitely added clarity. What he wanted to do was wrap those big hands of his around Arthur Tyrone's neck, and though she couldn't blame him, she certainly didn't want to act as Arthur's proxy.

"Really?" she asked, pacing backward again, even as her mind churned a thousand miles a second trying to find a way to turn the discussion to her advantage. It was a lucky break that they were now talking about Omnipotence, and with a little conversational skill she might just be able to introduce herself and then explain her plan. If he had this correspondence at his home, that probably meant he didn't want anyone in his office to know about the proposed takeover. Which also meant it would be wiser to speak with him here.

"Really!" he said. "But do you know what? The company's privately held. And it's one corporation inside another corporation that is hidden in another corporation. It's layer upon layer upon layer of bureaucracy, created, I'm sure, to hide the company's real owner. But I'll find him. And when I do…well, let's just say, he's not going to be very pleased to see me."

Perry cleared her throat. He'd just given her an avenue of entry. It wasn't a big avenue, it wasn't even a good avenue, but at least he'd finally given her a way to slowly slide the introduction of her true identity into the conversation, which she'd quickly lead into the explanation of her plan. "What makes you so sure the company's owner is a man? Or for that matter, just one person?"

He looked at her. "I'm not. In fact, I'm not sure of anything. Look at this," he said, holding the paper out so she could see it. "There's no address on this letterhead, no phone number, no fax. Just that one word and a silver and gold lightning bolt. Even if I wanted to get in touch with these people, even if I finally agreed to do what they wanted, I couldn't. You don't contact them. They contact you. To me, that's the ultimate in arrogance."

He tossed the letter to the desk, and Perry drew in a long breath. Despite the fact that Mike McGuire wasn't in the best frame of mind to hear this news, Perry knew it was now or never. She couldn't wait another second. Any minute now, his real baby-sitter could come knocking at the door and when she did, Perry would look guilty as a cat with feathers in its whiskers. Unless Perry explained that she wasn't the nanny his mother had hired and that her intentions were good, she didn't think Mike McGuire would kindly pause and listen attentively while she told him that she'd let him leave thinking she was the baby-sitter so she'd have a strategic advantage over him because she needed his help.

"Mr. McGuire," she began hesitantly.

"That's Mike," he said and turned away. "If you're going to be taking care of my children, you might as well call me by my first name. By the way, I'm sorry I yelled at you this morning. But I've been a little edgy lately."

"Oh, that's okay." Perry happily accepted his apology, seeing this as a wonderful turn of events. "You really didn't yell or anything like that. I mean, I could understand that you want your baby-sitter to be here on time...."

Obviously preoccupied, Mike leaned over the desk and began rummaging through the papers Perry had just moved around, then interrupted her as if she hadn't even been speaking. "Look, I only came back home because I forgot an editorial I'd written. So, please, don't feel like you have to stand here and talk to me, just get on with your business as if I weren't here."

"Well, actually, standing here talking to you *is* getting on with my business...."

"Having second thoughts already?"

"Uh, no. It's just that—"

"Oh, no," he said suddenly and bolted upright as if he'd been struck by the lightning on the Omnipotence letterhead. "They contacted you, didn't they?"

"No. I—"

"Well, it wouldn't surprise me. It didn't fool me for one minute when I found out Mrs. Martin and her husband suddenly had all the cash they needed to buy a new house in Florida and retire comfortably."

"Are you telling me you *know* somebody bribed your baby-sitter?"

"To throw me off guard, I think this company would do absolutely anything," he replied quietly. Then he glanced up at her and smiled in a way that was so self-depreciating it was charming. "Sounds ludicrous, doesn't it?"

"Yes, it does," Perry admitted, unwittingly smiling back at him. Not only did he have a beautiful, persuasive smile, he had the most incredible blue eyes, eyes that could melt your heart with softness or melt your limbs with fear. Quite obviously, he didn't care what anybody thought of him, because he never even attempted to stem his emotions. He just went with them. It was amazingly refreshing to meet a person who was so honest and genuine, particularly since everybody in her life tiptoed around her as if she were royalty. "But, it's encouraging to hear that you're not being fooled...."

"No. I'm not being fooled. Taken for a ride, yes. But fooled, no."

"Well, I'm sorry," Perry said, inching her way toward her introduction again, grateful that not only did she finally have her opening, but Mike McGuire also sounded reasonable. "That's why—"

"What do you have to be sorry about?" Mike asked, then shook his head as he laughed. "It's certainly not your fault that some huge conglomerate is trying to run my company out of business so they can hire me to do the same job—to run the same kind of company—except for them, not for myself."

"No, it's certainly not my fault, but—"

"Look, I hadn't intended to get into this with you so quickly but since we somehow veered into the subject, I want to warn you about what's going on here. These people bribed two of my advertising salespeople and one of my reporters into other jobs. Then, they very blatantly paid off my baby-sitter. And I have every reason in the world to believe they'll come after you, too. They may approach you right here at the house."

"Mr. McGuire," Perry said anxiously. Every time this man spoke, he gave her information she didn't have the right to hear at this point. Yet for some reason or other, she couldn't seem to get him to be quiet long enough to let her introduce herself. "Please, listen. I'm—"

"No, what I have to say is very important and I want *you* to listen. If anybody from that company sets one foot on my property, I want to know. I might not be able to stop them from stealing my employees, but I can certainly have them arrested for trespassing."

As he said the last, he pierced her with a look from his crystal-clear blue eyes and Perry knew beyond a shadow of a doubt that he meant business. Not only would he fight to the death if need be, using every weapon available, but he wouldn't be coerced into implementing a plan without being given every single detail of that plan, right down to why she created it. Arthur Tyrone may have met his match in Mike McGuire, and though Perry felt a certain stirring of pleasure from that knowledge, she also felt a quick quiver of stupidity. Cora had been right. It wasn't very realistic to think that she could simply appear on this man's doorstep and ask for his help, any more than it would be realistic to think she could introduce herself and not quickly discover what the inside of a small county jail cell looks like.

"Is that clear?"

"Perfectly," Perry said, then sent up a silent prayer that his real nanny wouldn't pick this precise moment to arrive. If she did, Perry had absolutely no idea how she'd explain herself.

"Good. I think I made a big mistake by not taking Mrs. Martin into my confidence. By the time she came to me with her resignation, it was easy to see that somehow the people from Omnipotence had made her believe she was justified in taking the money they'd offered. Despite the fact that I was pretty certain I knew what had happened, I also knew it was too late to try to reason with her."

As he spoke, he shoved aside a few more pieces of paper, then sighed with relief. "Here's my editorial." He folded the single sheet of paper into thirds, then stuffed it into the breast pocket of his jacket. "Look, all that information I gave you must stay confidential. There's only one other person aside from you who knows any of this, because I don't want to start a panic. So you have to promise me you won't breathe one word to anyone.''

Perry nodded.

"Give Mitzie a kiss for me. I've got to get going."

He turned and began walking out of the den. As Perry watched him go, her thoughts were warring between calling him back and explaining herself because it was the right, honest thing to do, and keeping her mouth shut to save her own hide. In the end, she stayed still and silent because she realized that the minute Mike McGuire discovered Perry was part owner of Omnipotence, the man wouldn't only have her arrested for trespassing, he'd have every justification to throw the book at her. She hadn't just entered his home, she'd let him leave without her having told him her true identity, she'd looked on his desk and allowed him to reveal information he wouldn't have revealed had he known who she really was.

She heard the sound of Mike McGuire's car engine at the same time that Mitzie came thumping into the den, wearing huge slippers that looked like stuffed bunnies and hugging her bear as if it were her best friend. "Did you find out how to make oatmeal?"

"Uh, no. I didn't get a chance to call yet."

"That's okay. We'll call now," Mitzie said, grabbing Perry's hand and pulling her toward the kitchen.

"Uh, Mitzie, why don't you go into the kitchen," Perry said, extracting her hand from the little girl's grasp. "And get everything ready to make the oatmeal." She did indeed intend to call Cora about the oatmeal, but there were a few other things she needed to discuss with Cora, and Perry decided that would best be done privately. Mitzie McGuire might only be four, but Perry wasn't taking any chances. She may not understand the things she heard Perry tell Cora, but she'd probably be able to repeat them. "And I'll call from in here."

After Mitzie nodded happily and made her way into the kitchen, Perry let herself fall into the chair beside the desk. She'd spent the night before driving to Ebensburg from Boston and the lack of sleep was beginning to catch up with her. She was tired, everything that could go wrong had gone wrong, her wonderful plan—the plan that would have saved Mike McGuire and trapped Arthur—was ruined and now she had absolutely no idea of what her next move should be.

Luckily, she was still thinking clearly enough to realize that she should use her phone card to make the call to Boston from Mike McGuire's phone. Because she didn't have her purse and didn't quite remember where she'd left it, she rose from the chair and walked into the kitchen where she discovered Mitzie had apparently lost patience and was pulling a box of doughnuts from a counter.

"You really are hungry, aren't you?" Perry asked with a laugh.

"My belly's growling," Mitzie said, smiling sheepishly.

"Well, I'll tell you what. It doesn't hurt to have a doughnut for breakfast every once in a while. How about if I get you a glass of milk?"

Pleased with that idea, Mitzie nodded and Perry retrieved a tall glass into which she poured a generous helping of milk, while Mitzie seated herself on one of the six captain's chairs around the rectangular oak table. Perry put the glass on the table, took a plate from another cupboard and set two fat, confectioners' sugar-covered doughnuts on the dish for Mitzie.

"It's not the most nutritious breakfast in the world, but it'll stop your growling."

Mitzie smiled joyfully, and content that Mitzie was not only being fed, but that she'd be occupied while Perry called Cora, Perry made her way out of the kitchen, into the entrance hall where she found her purse, through the living room and into the den again.

Using her phone card, she placed the call, then settled back on the chair next to the desk, grabbing a few seconds of rest while Cora's private line rang. Just as her eyelids began to droop closed, Cora answered her phone.

"Cora?" Perry gasped with relief. "Oh, God, am I glad to talk to you."

"What happened?" Cora asked anxiously.

"Oh, heavens. Everything," Perry groaned. "I got here and Mike McGuire thought I was his baby-sitter and yelled at me for being late. I let him leave under that assumption, thinking it would help to have him at something of a disadvantage when I finally did contact him, but he forgot something and returned to the house."

"And?"

"And he walked in on me reading a letter from Arthur."

"Oh, my gosh! Perry!"

"Cora, it all sounds stupid, but if you would have been here, you'd see it was perfectly innocent, and, actually a stroke of good luck. He ranted and raved for at least five minutes about Omnipotence, and from what he said, I didn't think it was wise to solicit his help at that point. But worse, if I would have given him my name in connection with Omnipotence, he could have discovered that Daddy's the man behind the whole conglomerate, and God only knows what he might have done with that information."

Cora blew her breath out on a long sigh. "Whew. I suppose we were lucky."

"Even though it doesn't sound like it, we were."

"I guess you're coming home, then."

Perry laughed miserably. "Eventually."

"Eventually?" Cora repeated curiously.

"Well, the real baby-sitter hasn't arrived yet." Even as she said the last, there was a knock at the door. "Wait a minute," Perry said, relieved to the point of sighing. "This is probably her now. Look, Cora, I don't think it's a good idea for you to hang on the line while I let this woman in."

"I'll get it!" Mitzie yelped and Perry heard the thump, thump, thump of her slippers as the little girl scampered down the hall.

"Mitzie's on her way to answer the door, so let's just hang up. I'll let this woman in, get her acclimatized, then call you from the first pay phone I find."

"Okay," Cora agreed. "But, Perry, make this quick. If I don't have to lie at that staff meeting this morning, I don't want to. It's much easier for me to say you're in New York shopping than to say you're taking an unexpected vacation. Particularly if you show up for work tomorrow morning."

"I understand. I'll get away as quickly as I can and then call you. Better yet, why don't you just stall? Try to hold off the start of that meeting...."

A shrill scream pierced the air and Perry's eyes bulged. "Oh, my God, Cora. I gotta go."

She jammed the receiver into its cradle and ran into the entryway where she found a beautiful brunette gaping at the two white confectioners' sugar handprints on the knees of her otherwise spotless black jumpsuit.

"What happened?" Perry asked, even as Mitzie flung herself at Perry, wailing as if someone had beaten her. Perry stooped to scoop her into her arms.

"She yelled at me," Mitzie sobbed at the same time that the brunette said, "That little brat attacked me."

Patting Mitzie's back for comfort, Perry faced the woman. "This child is not a brat," she clearly stated, scorching the tall, beautiful woman with a killer glare. "And I find it very hard to believe that she would attack anyone."

Obviously realizing her mistake, the woman took a long slow breath. "Look," she said, opening her hands in supplication, "my name is Robbin Farrington. I'm the woman Mary McGuire hired to be Mike McGuire's new housekeeper. I know I'm late, but that's only because I slept in. It will not happen again."

Perry took in the sight of the fashionable black jumpsuit, the strand of pearls around the woman's neck and her well-made-up face, and her eyebrows raised. Judging from the brunette's appearance, Perry would have guessed Robbin Farrington had spent the last two hours getting ready for work, and wondered why a housekeeper would find it essential to take the time to put on pearls and makeup to clean a house and take care of children. "Really?"

"Yes," Robbin said sweetly. "I worked for two families in the Alexandria, Virginia, area and I have wonderful references, which Mrs. McGuire checked thoroughly."

Perry inclined her head in agreement. "I'm sure she did."

"But I'm going to be candid with you and explain that I took this job very reluctantly."

Perry's eyebrows rose again. "I see."

"I'm sure you understand that because I'm very good at what I do and very much in demand, I can more or less set the rules...."

"Wait a minute," Perry said, stopping Robbin Farrington before she went any further. "What are you trying to say here?"

"Simply put?"

Perry nodded. "Simply put."

"Suggest to Mr. McGuire that he enroll that child in a day-care and I'll return tomorrow. If he doesn't wish to do that, please inform him that he can find himself another housekeeper."

"Well, Ms. Farrington," Perry said, slowly walking toward the front door, "thank you for your time." Using only one arm to hold Mitzie who had her arms wrapped securely around Perry's neck and her legs vised around Perry's waist,

Perry grabbed the doorknob. "This little girl is part of the job, and if you can't handle her, you're not wanted."

"Well, I never," Robbin Farrington huffed as Perry directed her out the door.

"No, I'm sure you haven't," Perry agreed, then closed the door behind her.

The next thirty seconds were filled with nothing but absolute silence. Perry stared straight ahead, watching dust dogs dance in the beam of light from the window off to the left. She'd just fired the baby-sitter Mike McGuire had labored almost a month to find, even though she had perfect justification for doing so.

He'd quite promptly have her arrested if he knew the truth.

Chapter Three

Perry called Cora again and told her to tell the staff she was in New York shopping. Then she bundled up Mitzie in tiny blue jeans, an even smaller shirt and tennis shoes that had Velcro strips for closures, knowing she didn't have any choice but to take Mike McGuire's daughter to him and quit her "job" as baby-sitter.

Because she couldn't explain why she'd come to his house this morning, why she'd stayed with Mitzie though she wasn't Mitzie's real sitter and why she'd allowed him to leave a second time without confessing her true identity, she had to carry out this charade to a realistic conclusion. The only alternative was to sever the relationship he thought existed in the typical way he would expect it to end. It wasn't going to be easy. It wasn't going to be honest. But it was the sole option available.

If only his mother hadn't hired the sitter, Perry could have simply spent the day with Mitzie and then disappeared this evening without explanation. But now she had to act fast.

Once Robbin Farrington spoke with Mike's mother, Mary McGuire would probably call Mike at his office and ask who the woman was who'd fired the baby-sitter. And unless Perry was already on her way back to Boston before all that happened, she'd be facing those angry blue eyes again and this time the anger would be justifiably directed at her.

The private investigator's report, which Perry had stashed under the front seat of her car gave the address of Mike McGuire's office. After several wrong turns in a town so small the business district was intermingled with the residences, Perry discovered that Mike McGuire's business wasn't in an office building, but rather a house converted to accommodate his newspaper.

She pulled into a parking space, unstrapped Mitzie from her seat belt, and, hand in hand, she and the quiet little girl walked up the sidewalk, Perry feeling as if she were going to her executioner, Mitzie hanging her head.

"Please don't tell Daddy I made the baby-sitter leave," Mitzie begged, tugging on Perry's hand when they reached the front door. "She scared me. She was like the witch in Snow White. She was going to hurt me."

Perry looked down at the frightened little girl and smiled reassuringly. "Remember what I told you? Neither one of us is going to mention that baby-sitter to your dad. Besides, you didn't make her leave. I did."

"I made her dress dirty," Mitzie mumbled guiltily.

"Yes, but she wasn't exactly innocent," Perry said, stooping to Mitzie's level so they could speak eye to eye. "I don't know what happened between the two of you, but it doesn't take a genius to figure out that grown-ups aren't supposed to argue with little kids."

Mitzie said nothing, merely stared at the planks of the wide porch.

"Mitzie," Perry said, lifting her chin, "do you understand that?"

Mitzie blinked twice, then she nodded.

"Good. You just do exactly what I told you. Don't say anything about that baby-sitter and let me handle your father."

Perry rose and again took Mitzie's hand. Reaching for the doorknob of the front door, she saw the small gold plaque that read *Star Tribune* and she smiled in spite of herself. If the size and stature of the sign was a foreshadowing of the size and stature of his business, Mike McGuire undoubtedly felt like David going against Goliath.

They entered the house and Perry discovered that most of the walls had been taken out of the first floor and the huge area that remained was filled with desks and chairs, blinking computer screens, file cabinets and noisy people. At the back of the room was a wall of windows with a doorway indicating another room, but horizontal blinds hid the office from view.

Holding Mitzie's hand, Perry walked up to the first desk. "Excuse me," she said quietly. "I need to speak with Mr. McGuire."

The young, blond receptionist looked up. "Well, hello, Mitzie," she said, her smile quick and genuine.

"Hi, Dolly," Mitzie said, still hanging her head.

"Uh-oh," Dolly said. "What's wrong?"

"Nothing," Perry assured quickly before Mitzie could say anything. "We just need to speak with Mr. McGuire."

"You and about fifty other people," Dolly said, smiling again. "Things are really jumping here today."

"I can see that," Perry agreed, looking around at all the activity bustling around her. Her father had been in the newspaper business since Perry was a baby, and Perry herself had joined the conglomerate the minute she graduated from college, but she'd never seen anything like this operation before. Rather than the sleek new machines, pristine offices and orderly desks to which Perry was accustomed, this office was a jumble of chaos and confusion.

"Why don't you two go back and wait in Mike's office and I'll tell him you're here? I think he's in the basement, working on the old printer. I should be able to have him up here in about five minutes."

Perry nodded and directed Mitzie toward the open door of the office with the horizontal blinds, as Dolly indicated. Inside, she took a seat on one of the two comfortable chairs, which sat in front of a huge, disorganized desk. Mitzie climbed into the other.

Even before they were settled, a short balding man bustled into the room. "Oh, excuse me," he said and began backing away.

"It's okay," Perry said, motioning for him to enter. "We're just waiting for Mr. McGuire."

"Uh-oh, Mitzie," the man said with a full-blown grin. "What'd you do now?"

Mitzie turned huge frightened blue eyes on Perry. "Nothing. Nothing at all," Perry said, noticing that Mitzie was squirming miserably, her face twisted with fear. Looking over at the man in the doorway again, she said, "Why does everybody automatically assume that Mitzie did something wrong?"

"Well," the man said and stepped into the office, "our little Mitzie here has a tendency to be a tad...well, spirited. By the way, I'm Sam," he added as he leaned against the desk Perry presumed to be Mike McGuire's. "I've been Mike's best friend for the past thirty years. There's nothing you can tell me about Mitzie that I haven't heard before."

Perry glanced at Mitzie again. The little girl's face was hidden by the curtain of her black hair as she hung her head in shame. "Mitzie's never been anything but a perfect angel with me," Perry said and Mitzie quickly looked up, rewarding Perry with a shy smile. "In fact," Perry added honestly, "she's the best little girl *I've* ever taken care of."

"That's wonderful," Sam said and slid down on the desk until it looked as if he was sitting on it rather than leaning against it. "I can see you're going to be a very good influence on her."

"A good influence on whom?" Mike McGuire asked, walking into the room. He might have been asking his staff member the question, but he was looking at Perry, once again skewering her with his unforgiving stare. Their gazes caught and held for several long seconds before Perry looked away, remembering she was supposed to be a housekeeper who no longer wanted her job, not an executive vice president of a multimillion-dollar conglomerate— so she couldn't act like one by staring down the opposition.

"Mitzie," Sam replied, easing himself off his boss's desk. "Your new housekeeper says Mitzie's the best little girl she's ever taken care of."

"What a relief." Even as he said the words, Perry looked at him and saw his frown become a slight smile, and his eyes change from icy blue to a tepid hue as bright and as warm as a morning sky, and, feeling her first twinge of guilt, Perry looked away again. She managed a fifty-person department for the corporate offices of Omnipotence and wasn't afraid, intimidated or even slightly confused by anyone. Yet this man only had to look at her and Perry felt things she'd never felt before.

Guilty. Good Lord, why should she feel guilty? She'd tried to explain who she was at least five times, but *he* stopped her. *He* left her. *He* would imprison her. This little charade wasn't her fault, but his, and, dammit, she didn't have any options left.

"When Dolly told me you were here, I was positive it was because Mitzie had done something wrong," Mike said.

His words brought Perry out of her reverie and she noticed that he'd dealt with Sam, dismissed him and then seated himself behind his messy desk. "Oh, no, Mitzie's fine," Perry said.

"Really? Then what other reason could you possibly have to go to the trouble of finding my office?"

Frowning, she said, "It wasn't any trouble to find this place. In fact, it was easy."

His gaze caught hers and held. "I never gave you the address."

"Oh," she said, finally catching his meaning. "Your address is on your letterhead. I caught a glimpse of it while I was looking for the phone book," Perry admitted as Mitzie scampered off her seat and ran to her father, who immediately scooped her into his arms and settled her on his lap. Though it had been Perry's intention to jump right into announcing her resignation, the father-and-daughter interaction beat her to the punch.

"So, you're being a good girl today?" Mike asked his daughter and Mitzie glanced sheepishly at Perry. Perry nodded slightly as an indicator that Mitzie could say she was.

"I had doughnuts for breakfast," she announced happily.

"That's wonderful!" Mike said, then laughed with glee as he hugged his little girl. Still smiling, he looked at Perry. "You don't know how good it is to have a baby-sitter come in with good news instead of bad."

"Did your old baby-sitter bring Mitzie in often?" Perry asked curiously, so caught up in Mitzie's problems that she'd temporarily forgotten her own. She'd never before seen a person who so quickly and so easily assumed guilt. Or a person whom everybody so quickly and so easily assumed was guilty. The poor child hadn't even done anything—except smear a *nasty* woman's jumpsuit with sugar.

"The first baby-sitter only brought Mitz in about once a week," Mike said, leaning back into his chair while Mitzie cuddled into his chest. "But Mrs. Martin was here every other day. I never really figured out if Mitzie misbehaved that much or if Mrs. Martin was just too old to handle a child this young. Anyway, with everything else that's going on today, the last thing I needed to hear was that Mitzie hadn't wasted a minute to start misbehaving for you."

Looking at the happy father and daughter who sat cuddled together on the tall-backed office chair, Perry shifted uncomfortably. Her resignation was supposed to be swift and simple, but she had the distinct impression that the reasons for it would quickly, easily, immediately, get blown out of proportion based on Mitzie's reputation. A reputation Perry wasn't really sure the poor kid deserved. But unless Perry thought of a good reason for quitting this job that didn't involve Mitzie, the child would get the blame.

She cleared her throat. "Yes, well, Mitzie's been very well behaved for me, but I have to tell you that I'm not—"

In that precise second, the phone rang and Mike answered it automatically. "Hello...what?" he yelped into the receiver. "But I just fixed that! Oh, no," he groaned miserably.

Mitzie slid off her father's lap, scampered around the desk and leaped to Perry's lap. She pressed her little hands to Perry's cheeks before she reached up and placed a smacking kiss on Perry's lips. "Let's go home," she said, smiling happily.

"Honey, we can't go home," Perry whispered, then hugged Mitzie as the little girl snuggled into Perry's neck with a contented sigh. "Perry's got to go to her real home, and in order to go home I have to talk to your father...."

"But we didn't play yet."

"I know, honey, but..."

Mike disconnected his call and the second the receiver hit the cradle, the phone began ringing again. "Now what?" he thundered without even saying hello. "Oh, hello," he said more calmly, and, cuddling Mitzie, Perry settled into her chair with a heavy sigh, feeling guilty again, even though she knew she shouldn't. He was every bit as culpable for this misunderstanding as she was, Perry thought.

"Well, that was my mother," Mike said, returning the phone's receiver to its cradle. Perry didn't even have the chance to register the fear that resulted from that piece of news because Mike continued to talk happily. "She wanted to make sure you'd arrived and things were going well because she's going out of town for the day."

"She is?" Perry asked quickly, relief pouring through her like rich red wine. Now there was no way Robbin Farrington would be able to reach Mary McGuire to complain about being fired!

"Yes, just shopping in Pittsburgh. She'll be back tomorrow night."

And maybe Robbin Farrington would be back in Alexandria, Virginia, by then, Perry thought, blinking rapidly. With the urgency of the situation gone, Perry's mind again became focused and directed. There was no sense in risking Mitzie's reputation based on a decision made in haste. A wise woman would step back and think about all this, because nine chances out of ten, there was a good way out of this situation. And she had all day to think of it.

"Now," Mike said, bringing Perry out of her reverie. "What can I do for you?"

Perry took a deep breath. "Actually," she said, smiling sheepishly, "I just wanted to take a drive down here and see if I could find your office. You know, just in case there's ever an emergency and I have to come here."

Without so much as a word of comment, Mike McGuire stared at her, his blue eyes fixed on her so tightly, Perry's heart stopped. In the paralyzing seconds that followed, half of her became terrified that he realized she wasn't telling him the whole truth, and the other half felt strangely hypnotized, unable to pull her eyes away, even though it would be much more comfortable to do so. For a second she toyed with the idea of telling him his mother had made the suggestion that she locate his office for future reference, because she knew the mention of his mother would allay his suspicions. But pretending to know his mother would really turn this whole situation into the kind of lie from which she'd never recover, and, save her hide or not, she couldn't convince herself to do it. Then he smiled and Perry's heart started beating again.

"Oh. Okay. That's a good idea."

Sighing with relief, Perry rose. "I can see you're busy, so we'll just go now."

"Okay," Mike agreed and rose, too. "We'll see you tonight, then."

"Yes," Perry said, and felt another twinge of guilt. She hadn't solved this problem, she'd only prolonged it, but she did have a whole day to try to figure out a way to make everybody happy. "We'll see you tonight."

"I couldn't help it, Cora. I couldn't very well quit after I learned Mitzie had had such a bad relationship with the last housekeeper. The whole darned office was expecting her to have done something wrong, and she was scared to death. If I would have quit, no matter what excuse I gave, everybody would have automatically assumed Mitzie was to blame."

"Your heart's too soft."

"Yeah, well, now what do I do?"

"I haven't the slightest idea, Ms. Pierson," Cora responded irritably. "I was just going to ask you the same thing."

"Well, you can tell the staff I'm still in New York," Perry answered, stretching the phone cord to its limit as she paced the kitchen. Stuffed with a burger from a fast-food restaurant, Mitzie was comfortably napping on the couch. "While I sit here in Pennsylvania trying to figure out a good story for Mike McGuire that won't get Mitzie in trouble, or me arrested for impersonating a baby-sitter."

"At this point, Perry, I'm tempted to tell you, you deserve anything you get."

"Why? Because I rescued a little girl from a woman she referred to as the wicked witch in 'Snow White'?"

"No, because you haven't told the man the truth yet."

"Cora, I can't tell him the truth. Unfortunately, I can't think of *anything* to tell him."

"Well, then, it looks like you have yourself a full-time job."

Perry started to laugh at Cora's joke, but as quickly as her laughter came, it died. "Wait a minute, Cora. That's a great idea."

"What?" Cora asked suspiciously.

Perry began to chuckle again. "Oh, Cora, this is wonderful."

"What's wonderful?"

"This job. Don't you see? It's the perfect opportunity. The papers for Mike McGuire's employment proposal from Omnipotence are here, in his den at the house, probably because he doesn't want his staff to find them. So, if I stay here, acting as his baby-sitter/housekeeper, not only will I have access to them, but while we're eating dinner, or something, I could probably get him to talk about everything Arthur's ever said and done. We could get everything we need to implicate Arthur, and we wouldn't have to embarrass the company or my father."

"You're crazy."

"I'm serious, Cora."

"It sounds good in theory, Perry, except for one thing."

"What's that?"

"How do you expect to work as a housekeeper when you've never even rinsed out a glass in your entire life?"

"Well, I was sort of hoping you could help me with that."

Mitzie entered the room just then, her tiny blue jeans unzipped, her T-shirt inside out and backward, with its tag brushing Mitzie's milk-white chin. But she was smiling, beaming actually, as she wrapped herself around Perry's legs and hugged her with all her might.

"Even if I Federal Express the cook to you, it won't do you one darned bit of good if Robbin Farrington calls Mike's mother."

"I don't really think she's going to do that. After all, she called Mary McGuire's granddaughter a brat, and she said she took this job with reservations. My guess is she's probably on the interstate right now, barreling back to Alexandria."

"You hope."

"Actually, the more I think about it, the more sure I am. I don't know how Mary McGuire talked her into taking this job, but Robbin didn't want it. That was pretty obvious."

"Okay, then, what are you going to do if Mike figures out who you are?"

"How is he going to figure out who I am?" Perry asked, smiling at Mitzie. "Cora, the man doesn't suspect a thing, so there's no reason for him to go snooping to figure out who I am. Besides, he has enough problems and he's not going to go looking for trouble. He needs me."

"Fat chance! Perry, what he needs is a housekeeper. How in the devil do you plan to hide the fact that you can't cook, clean or iron?"

"Well, I'll call you every day and tell you what I need to do, and you just tell me how to do it."

"Perry, this really is not as simple as you're trying to make it out to be. Housekeeping . . ."

"Please. I'm in now, Cora, and no one suspects a thing. If we don't take advantage of this opportunity, we may just be throwing away our chance to catch Arthur in the act."

When Perry used that tone of voice, Cora cringed. Well aware that Perry wouldn't hear her objections if she voiced them, Cora fell into the tall-backed chair behind her desk and rubbed her hand across her forehead. "All right. I want to see Arthur exposed as much as you do, but, Perry, don't kid yourself. This isn't going to be easy."

"I know, but you have to admit, it's still a golden opportunity. We can't just throw it away because I've never made a bed. Besides, it'll be worth it." Reattaching the Velcro strip on Mitzie's tennis shoe, she smiled at Mitzie and winked. Mitzie began to giggle.

"Okay," Cora said, then she sighed. "We'll take this one step at a time. Just look around and tell me what's dirty."

Perry glanced at the sinkful of dishes, the spots on the yellow linoleum floor, the papers piled on the white Formica countertops. She cleared her throat. "Actually, Cora, everything's dirty."

"Oh, boy," Cora said. A few seconds passed in absolute silence and finally she sighed. "Okay, here's how we'll handle this. Get a piece of paper and a pencil because you're going to need to write some things down. First, we'll take care of the cooking because any man will be fairly reasonable as long as he's not hungry. I want you to go to a grocery store and find something that's already cooked, something frozen. . . ."

Cora proceeded to give Perry brand names, which she recommended highly, then instructed her to read the directions on the packages carefully and follow them to the letter. She suggested certain products to aid with scrubbing and dusting, then—with a sigh—explained the difference between scrubbing and dusting. At Perry's groan of disgust, Cora suggested that it might be a good idea to buy a pair of rubber gloves and wear them at all times when doing housework.

Last but not least, Cora also volunteered that if Perry recognized she couldn't do any more than dust and run the vacuum cleaner before her employer got home, all she had to do was hide small bowls of pine cleaner in strategic places and turn the lights down, because the clean smell of the house would keep her employer from investigating, and the dim lights would prevent him from seeing the obvious.

Chapter Four

The minute Mike McGuire entered his house, the scent of pine cleaner hit him. He breathed it in appreciatively. His house hadn't even gotten a lick and a promise in a month. Mrs. Martin had quit then, and his mother had agreed to baby-sit his kids, but only at her house and not indefinitely. For at least three weeks, he'd advertised, asked and even tried begging, but not one soul in his little community wanted Mrs. Martin's old job. It seemed a miracle when his mother told him she'd discovered the perfect replacement through the friend of a friend of one of her pinochle partners.

Ambling down the dark entrance hall to the kitchen, Mike listened to the sounds of silence. The dim light didn't bother him nearly as much as the quiet. Even when Mitzie was in her sullen mood, the boys were generally screaming.

He entered the kitchen, which he'd left in shambles, and when he switched on the light, his eyebrows rose in surprise. There was absolutely nothing on any of the countertops. The stove was immaculate. The refrigerator sparkled. Even the floor was clean.

Not bad. Not bad at all.

As he walked a little farther into the room, he saw a note on the table. "We went to the Coopers'," was all it said. It was signed by the boys. Janette and Paul Cooper raised beagles, so Mike wasn't surprised, but he was still angry they weren't around.

Stripping off his suit coat, Mike looked around. Well, the kitchen was clean and the note explained the twins, but where were the housekeeper and Mitzie? And where was supper? He dropped his coat to a captain's chair and headed for the door at the back of the kitchen.

Though he didn't turn on the light, he could tell the dining room had been vacuumed. The walnut table polished to the point that it reflected the light gliding in from the kitchen. There were no books, no papers, no dishes on the buffet or in the hutch.

The woman was certainly thorough. Unfortunately, she also wasn't around.

He walked through the dining room and into the den, which hadn't been vacuumed, and had probably forgotten what a dust cloth looked like. The papers that had been on the dining-room table and in the hutch, were now on his desk, as were the mail and an odd assortment of things belonging to the twins. Well, what did he expect? She had to put things somewhere. And she wouldn't have any way of knowing where he kept anything since he hadn't told her. Hell, he'd hardly even spoken to her, not even when she was nice enough to come into his office. He was so damned preoccupied with his business and its problems, and so damned anxious to get the housework off his mind, he hadn't given her one word of instruction. Not even about Mitzie. Not even to warn her about Mitzie.

He drew a deep breath and switched off the light. On Saturday, they could sit down together and he'd explain his filing system.

His next destination was the living room and he stopped only one foot inside the door. There on the huge overstuffed couch of yellow, rust and peach-flowered print lay his new housekeeper, sound asleep. The faint glow of a brass lamp was the only light in the room, but even in the semi-darkness, Mike could tell this room, like the den, was still a mess.

Cautiously, he tiptoed to the couch, but before he attempted to awaken her, he stopped himself. In his whole life, he'd ever seen anybody look so tired. In fact, she looked as if she hadn't slept in days. Her perfect chignon of this morning was in straggly disarray, with locks falling from their pins and going in every direction. Her peachy complexion was smudged with dirt and her jogging suit—of the ugliest shade of rose imaginable—was also filthy. He laughed at the too-big rubber gloves.

He hunkered down beside her. So where was the sophisticate who'd knocked at his door this morning? he wondered, letting one finger glide along a wayward strand of strawberry-blond hair. That woman had looked as if she didn't know which end of a broom swept, and he'd questioned why she'd even want a job as a housekeeper, let alone how she planned on cleaning while dressed in a suit so pale and so pretty that two minutes in his kitchen would destroy it. Now, here she lay, dressed the way a housekeeper should be dressed, filthy dirty and apparently tired—but still incredibly beautiful.

He raised a hand to her shoulder and shook gently. "Wake up..."

He stopped, lifted his eyes heavenward and sighed. In all the confusion, his mother had forgotten to give him the housekeeper's name, and he'd been so relieved she found someone, he'd forgotten to ask.

Nonetheless, his housekeeper answered him. "What?" she croaked, scratching a finger through the hair at her temple.

"You have to get up," he said softly, smiling because she made such a picture lying there, still wearing rubber gloves.

"What time is it, Cora? Can't I sleep another hour or so?" she mumbled, nestling into the fat orange pillow on which her head rested. Her hair spilled out and fell over one shoulder as she rubbed her nose with her glove-covered hand and grimaced—probably from the pungent odor of the pine cleaner—but she didn't open her eyes and it was obvious she wasn't actually awake yet. Light from the brass lamp made shadows that mingled with the long black lashes of her closed eyes and kissed the peachy glow of her cheeks.

She *was* beautiful, Mike thought, smothering another smile. His finger edged up toward her wayward hair again, but in the last second before he touched her smooth skin, it hit him. Why would this beautiful woman arrive at his house dressed stunningly, rather than dressed to work?

Why? And suddenly, the reason dawned on him.

His mother had set one of her *matchmaking* schemes into motion by conniving the daughter or niece or cousin of a friend into taking this job. Now Mary McGuire was sitting back expecting the shared housekeeping experiences or child-rearing to work some kind of magic that would throw them into eternal bliss.

Oh, brother! he thought, stifling his anger. It all made perfect sense. That's why his mother hadn't given him this woman's name—he'd recognize it! Mary McGuire had probably once tried to get him to take this woman out on a blind date!

Lord, he was stupid.

"Where's Mitzie?" he asked, not quite sure how he was going to deal with this woman or his mother.

"Who?"

"Mitzie," he repeated, this time a little louder.

"Mitzie who?" she grumbled.

"Mitzie, my daughter, that's who!" Mike thundered, furious not only that his child might be uncared for, but that this woman was so irresponsible, she didn't even remember Mitzie, let alone know where she was. If this wasn't proof positive this woman wasn't a housekeeper, nothing was.

Her brown eyes flew open. "Mitzie," she gasped. "She was taking a nap!"

"What time did you put her to sleep?" Mike demanded angrily as he pushed himself to his feet.

"I . . . I don't know. About four, I guess."

He took a deep breath to stop his anger. This was neither the time nor the place to handle the problem. Once the kids were fed and in bed, he and this woman would have a heart-to-heart chat. And he'd send her packing. But for now, he'd just let well enough alone. "Okay, don't worry about it. I'll go get her right now, while you start supper."

Perry blinked. "Uh, since I, um, fell asleep," she stammered, stopping as Mike began to walk out of the room, "why don't I just make something simple? This afternoon, I found some ravioli in the freezer. . . ."

"You did?" He turned, faced her and bestowed upon her a look of total confusion.

"Uh, yeah," she said, shrugging. "I'll just cook that and heat up some spaghetti sauce. There was some broccoli, too," she ventured.

Mike had no idea what this woman was trying to pull, but he did know there had not been any frozen ravioli in his freezer. Had there been, he would have cooked it instead of twice taking the kids out to eat the day before. His gaze locked with hers for several seconds but he didn't say anything, he merely turned and stormed out of the living room.

Perry breathed a sigh of relief. The day had been one minor disaster after another, yet somehow everything always fell into place. First, she had to shop for clothes to wear for cleaning and discovered that the stores didn't have salespeople to help her choose. She had to find her purchases herself. And go through a line to pay for them.

At the grocery store, Mitzie talked Perry into buying more junk food than was humanly possible for one person to carry, and Perry almost panicked. But out of an aisle stepped a blond-haired, green-eyed clerk, who—after greeting Mitzie—announced that she was Janette Cooper, a neighbor of Mike's, and that she'd happily help Perry carry her bags to her car.

Greatly relieved, Perry followed Janette Cooper to the parking lot, only to realize she'd forgotten where she parked her car and, carrying four bags of groceries, Perry led a talkative neighbor and a whining four-year-old from one end of the parking lot to the other, until she finally found her car.

As she guided herself through this strange world where people shopped in long, flat stores that carried everything, not just dresses, or shoes, or leather goods, Perry had encountered disaster after disaster, but each time, somebody came to her rescue. Now fate had unwittingly handed her the perfect way out tonight.

All afternoon, she'd despaired about Mike McGuire's reaction to food that was obviously store-bought, no matter how good it tasted, and she'd been concerned for nothing. He might not be happy about eating a frozen dinner of sorts, but because she'd fallen asleep, he wasn't questioning why he had to. Though Perry would much prefer to know what she was doing instead of stumbling out of all her predicaments, because luck happened to be at her side, she didn't have much say in the matter. She was in a totally foreign environment, and because of that, she knew she was creating her own problems. It hadn't taken her long to realize learning how to live in this rural community was going to be as much of a problem as learning how to cook and clean; she just hoped that after all that, she'd have enough energy to carry on a conversation with Mike McGuire so she could get the goods on Arthur.

Perry studied the directions for the ravioli to the point that she knew them by heart, but that didn't help her get the lid off the jar of spaghetti sauce. When Mitzie jubilantly arrived in the kitchen, it was to see Perry struggling to open a jar that obviously wanted to stay closed.

"Hey, Dad," Mitzie yelled. "Perry can't get the lid off."

Mike strode into the room and snatched the jar from Perry's hands without a word. Swallowing, Perry backed away from him. Good Lord, he was big. As he struggled with the jar lid, she took a quick glance from his feet to the top of his head and guessed he was at least six feet tall.

His forearm flexed as he twisted the lid and Perry swallowed again. He had muscles. That was it. He had real muscles, like a person who did more than sit behind a desk and run a newspaper. He looked like a lumberjack, or an iron worker or a mason. Not that she cared what he did for a living, but truth be known, Perry was realizing she was afraid of him. And why shouldn't she be? She didn't know this man from Adam and she was about to try to get him to tell her the most private affairs of his business; and to do that, she had to fool him into thinking she was competent to take care of his most prized possession, his kids.

"Here, already!"

The gruff command issued by the man shoving a jar of spaghetti sauce into her hands brought Perry out of her reverie. Silently, she took the proffered liquid and inched toward the cupboard, which she now knew held pots and pans.

"Don't you think that damned ravioli's boiled long enough?" he yelled as he punched the buttons of the telephone. "Janette, tell those boys of mine to get home!" He slammed the receiver into its cradle and stormed to the refrigerator. "I'll do the salad. You take care of that ravioli."

The mood of her new employer was enough to turn Perry's knees to rubber—and make her question every decision she'd made since walking into his house this morning—but as she pivoted to grab a pot holder, she saw the strange look Mitzie leveled at her dad. Her head was tilted so far, her black locks hung to her waist, and the question in her eyes answered all of Perry's fears. Mike McGuire normally didn't act like this with his family. He might be a tyrant with his employees and the bear of the office, but at home he was generally even-tempered.

Still, dinner was eaten in silence. The boys, Timmy and Tommy, red-haired, freckle-faced, ten-year-old twins, received a severe reprimand and a strict punishment for leaving on a school night, and from that point on, nobody dared to speak. Nonetheless, Perry ate heartily. She couldn't decide if she was so hungry, her ravioli tasted good, or if the frozen meal really was as tasty as it seemed to be. In any event, silent and somewhat content, she stuffed herself.

But it wasn't until the boys went to their room to do homework and Mitzie was sent to the living room to watch TV, that Mike started thinking clearly. His mother, bless her heart, really did have his best interests in mind. And she'd vowed to give up matchmaking a year ago. Blaming her for this was like accusing his mother of lying. Which he did not want to do.

Giving Perry the benefit of the doubt, he had to admit she'd dealt very well with a filthy house and three strange kids, despite the fact that the three times he'd seen her today, he was so preoccupied with his business that he hadn't thought to give her information, and might have even missed a question or two. When she discovered the cupboards were bare, she might have realized it was pointless to call him for help and simply solved the problem on her own. Once he mentioned to her that he knew there had been no food in the house, she'd probably laugh and tell him how much he owed her for the shopping trip. He was just a tad too sensitive because his mother was *always* trying to find a new wife for him. And the whole setup, pretty housekeeper, clean kitchen, mysteriously discovered food in his freezer, all looked like something his mother would cook up.

"I'm going to reimburse you for the food," he announced suddenly into the silence after the kids left the kitchen.

"It's all right," Perry said, shrugging. "I was the one who was hungry for ravioli," she lied easily, but as it always did when she told an untruth, her face flamed with color. "I'll pay for it."

At that, he laughed. "You took this job to make money, not spend it," he reminded her. "So, I'll reimburse you for the ravioli," he insisted, smiling.

Little lights twinkled in his blue eyes and for a minute, Perry stared at him. It was funny that she couldn't stop noticing how handsome he was. He didn't have the kind of looks a model had, and neither would she recommend him for the movies, but he had a definite male attractiveness to his face. His nose had probably been broken, but it wasn't malformed, just a bit crooked. His lips were full, not thin, flat lines, and his hair was such a shiny black that Perry got the sudden urge to touch it.

"How much was the ravioli?"

That time his voice was a little gruffer and Perry frowned. She was tired, stuffed and still had to face a sink full of dirty dishes. She didn't feel like a game of one-upmanship over money. "It's no problem, really."

"I like to pay for my children's food."

That time, his voice was downright angry and Perry's heart thumped to a stop. This wasn't like dinner at the club. To Mike McGuire, the purchase of food had nothing to do with one-upmanship.

"Oh."

"How much was the ravioli?"

"Uh, uh," Perry stammered. She hadn't looked at individual price tags. She decided she didn't want to know.

"I don't know," she conceded with a grimace.

Closing his eyes, Mike decided one last time to be patient with her. If he asked her again and she didn't tell him, he was going to fire her. Not because this proved his mother had sent her. No, this was starting to look like his father's handiwork. A man who stuffed twenties in between the cushions of the couch and left tens behind the aspirin could hire a woman and feed her money to keep his son's house running—particularly since his son's business had unexpectedly fallen upon hard times. He could also be as guilty as a mother who pointed out attractive women at church. It was beginning to look as if either of his parents could have sent this woman to him, and if they had, somebody better be ready for a fight.

Harnessing his anger, he asked in a voice that was dangerously quiet, "How much was the ravioli?"

"Actually," Perry said, swallowing at the severity of his tone, "I don't know. I bought a bunch of things."

"How much was the bunch of things?" he inquired reasonably.

"It came to $127.50."

"Did you say $127.50? What did you do? Shop for a week?"

"No, I bought a lot of bananas and after-school snacks." The last was a rationalization she'd conjured up as she stowed the chips and other goodies in the pantry earlier today.

"Okay, I'll write out a check," he said, heaving a sigh.

"Oh, but, I bought those snacks. I'll pay for them," Perry insisted good-naturedly. "I'm the one who couldn't resist Mitzie's manipulation, so I'll pay the price."

"Mitzie is my daughter, so *I'll* pay the price," Mike said quietly. "But that does bring up an interesting question. If you're so in need of money that you accept a job nobody else wants, how can you afford to pay for over a hundred dollars' worth of potato chips?"

Holding back a groan, Perry realized she'd made another major error. Paying for the groceries wasn't just a matter of pride, it was a real social issue here. How you spent your money in this little town could tell a lot about your personality. And instead of her kindness appearing to be a kindness, it was making her look as suspicious as the beam of a flashlight in a dark, deserted office.

To stall for time before answering his question, Perry rose from her chair, but Mike's hand shot out to grab her wrist. Looking at the large hand with long, tapered fingers, Perry swallowed again. Everything she'd said and done in the past fifteen hours had been absolutely, positively wrong. And this conversation was turning out to be no exception. She was almost afraid to answer the question, but she knew Mike McGuire wasn't going to let her walk away until she did.

"I'm from out of town. How was I supposed to know no one else wanted this job?"

The fingers grasping her arm tightened, albeit only slightly, and Perry knew he didn't believe her, or if he did, he wasn't happy about her answer. He twisted her arm around, and as he did, he examined her hands. Perry followed his line of vision and tried to see her hand through his eyes. It was a tiny hand with slender fingers and long, well-manicured fingernails. It was a hand that looked as if it hadn't worked a day in its life, and until today, it hadn't.

Oh, why had she bought those rubber gloves?

"What did you do before you came here?" he demanded evenly. "You certainly weren't a housekeeper."

"Actually, I worked for a hospital." And she did. Every year, she organized the charity ball sponsored by her father's corporation to raise money for the religious hospital that never seemed to have enough funds. It wasn't a complete lie; in reality, it wasn't a lie at all. It was simply an omission of fact to save her skin.

"As what?"

"I was in administration."

He brought his blue eyes up to look into her brown ones. One of his bushy black eyebrows arched as he studied her face. "The perfect experience to become a housekeeper," he said with a disgusted frown as he loosened the pressure on her arm.

Despite the fact that he was letting her go, real fear rolled over Perry as she felt her slim chance of catching Arthur drift away from her. If she didn't think of something and think of it quickly, this man wasn't going to let her stay, then she'd never catch Arthur. Mike McGuire might save himself, but there was no guarantee Arthur's next victim would be as smart and as determined as Mike. And no guarantee she'd find an avenue into the next person's life that would enable her to rescue him or her.

"Look, you might as well know," Perry said, her voice coming out on a quiver. It was fairly obvious he knew she wasn't a housekeeper looking for a housekeeping job, but there were other ways to make her presence here believable. "I'm not a housekeeper at all, I'm just a woman who got really bored with her job and her life and went looking for a change of scenery, and this seemed like the perfect opportunity.''

Her host cursed softly under his breath, running his free hand through his black hair in frustration. ''Oh, boy,'' he groaned. ''Hundreds of thousands of women in our country are migrating away from the home, particularly away from housework, and you expect me to believe you voluntarily chose the opposite?''

Clearing her throat, Perry glanced down at her clean plate. For some reason, it didn't seem all that farfetched to her. There were days she wouldn't mind chucking the office and spending the rest of her life at home. ''Yes.''

Mike said, ''Oh, boy,'' again, but this time he looked at the ceiling as he ran his fingers through his coal black hair. His mother was behind this, he knew it. But he didn't have a sitter, and this Perry—Perry whose name he knew only because Mitzie constantly used it—genuinely seemed to want this job. And the kids liked her....

''How about if we establish a trial period?''

''A trial period?''

''Sure, all new employees are usually on probation for say, thirty or sixty days.''

Perry looked down at him. Her beautiful brown eyes were wet and shiny, but not from tears. Her eyes were naturally radiant. And even in the bright light of the kitchen, her complexion was clear and flawless. Peachy. Smooth.

''Are you telling me that you could fire me at any time during the first thirty or sixty days?''

Mike cleared his throat. ''Well, sixty days is a bit much.''

''I don't want to spend even the first *thirty* days worrying about how I'll explain to Mitzie that you don't want me around anymore if you choose to fire me on day twenty-nine.''

It surprised him so much that this woman thought about Mitzie's feelings, not her own, that Mike simply stared at her. Even if his mother had planted Perry, she wasn't faking her feelings for his baby girl. He'd realized she'd formed some kind of a bond this morning when she changed her mind about reporting whatever it was Mitzie had done that caused her to bring his daughter into his office, and then covered for Mitzie at the last minute instead of demand she be punished. No matter how much he didn't want to be a part of a matchmaking scheme, he did want a baby-sitter who'd take good care of Mitzie. And there was no doubt in his mind this woman would take excellent care of Mitzie.

Mike sat back in his chair. "Okay, you're right, but that doesn't mean we shouldn't have any probationary period at all."

"Agreed, but I don't think it should be any longer than two weeks."

Mike considered that. Could two weeks be enough time to subtly squelch his mother's plan without offending the first baby-sitter who hadn't once yelled at him for the messy house? The first baby-sitter who actually thought about Mitzie's feelings before her own? And the first baby-sitter who wasn't afraid of the twins?

It would have to be. Because if he couldn't somehow let this woman know he had no intention of marrying her—no matter what his mother might have promised—he'd have to fire her.

It was that simple.

Chapter Five

Mike opened his bedroom door and breathed a heavy sigh of relief. He did that every night after he finally got the twins and Mitzie to sleep. So tonight was nothing special. The kids hadn't been any better or worse than normal. He only hoped the new baby-sitter understood that.

She'd disappeared right after Mitzie was in pajamas, and though she hadn't seemed upset or angry, she left without a word of goodbye. In fact, Mike hadn't even realized she was leaving.

He closed the door with a soft, almost silent click, so he wouldn't awaken anybody, then padded quietly to the bed and sat on the edge of the green quilt, which Elaine had bought from a roadside vendor in Lancaster.

With another sigh, he raised one foot and removed its sock, then repeated the process with his second foot.

He didn't ever think of Elaine anymore. He didn't really want to think about a woman who'd desert her husband and her three kids, particularly since one of those kids was still an infant at the time. But tonight for some reason, thoughts of Elaine—strange, almost imperceptible thoughts of Elaine—would hit him and then disappear about as fast as they came.

Tonight he needed to go to bed early. His business was being pursued by an unscrupulous shark, he'd hired a housekeeper who appeared to be a sure plant of his meddling mother, his household was still disrupted from the loss of his old housekeeper, and just when he least expected it tonight, he'd get a flash of memory. Velvety skin, sweet-smelling hair, soft feminine sweaters.

And he didn't want to deal with it. He'd dealt with it for over three years. Well, actually, he'd dealt with those memories for two years, then he'd wisened up, whipped himself into shape and hadn't spent a miserable, lonely night since. He simply convinced himself that there might be a gender difference for other people, but as far as he was concerned, there was no such thing as men and women. Only people inhabited this planet.

After removing his shirt and trousers, Mike piled all the pillows into a haphazard stack, then reached for the techno-thriller he had stashed under his bed.

No, he didn't want to think about Elaine tonight. He didn't want to think of soft skin, or silky hair, or any of those things. He opened his book.

He read for only ten minutes before his eyelids began to droop. Raising his gaze from his reading, he took a long, slow breath and found himself staring at the bathroom door just as the baby-sitter slid out from behind it, wrapped only in a huge bath towel. Her skin held a pink hue as if it had been well buffed with terry cloth. Her hair was tied in a ponytail at the top of her head, but strawberry-blond ringlets framed her face. The scent of bath oils or bubble bath permeated the room.

It was then Mike realized he hadn't been thinking of Elaine all day. He'd been thinking of Perry. His definition of femininity had almost immediately been replaced by a woman he'd known less than twenty-four hours. And now she was standing before him pink and naked, wrapped in a fluffy towel and smelling like every man's version of heaven.

"What the..."

Within three seconds he was off his bed and scrambling for his robe.

Perry screamed. Half from fright—seeing someone you don't expect always scares you—and half from the shock of Mike's near nakedness. It never occurred to her that she had less clothes on than he did. It never occurred to her to be embarrassed. She didn't, couldn't think about herself at all. The sight of his muscular, hairy, half-naked body just about floored her.

As he turned and stretched to grab his robe from the chair beside the window, Perry got a flash of shiny red boxer shorts and long, hair-covered legs. The skin of his smooth back and broad shoulders glowed in the lamplight. When he turned to face her, tying the robe's cloth belt at his waist, she saw a handful of crisp black hair hugging his collar and two incredibly hairy arms poking out of three-quarter-length sleeves.

"What are you doing here?" he asked, sounding as if his patience had been strained to its limit and this was the final straw.

Perry took a deep breath, rolling the knot at her breasts into a tight ball. Her skin was dry, so the cool, early-September air had nothing to do with raising gooseflesh on her exposed limbs. Finding her employer lying on her bed in a pair of skimpy red boxer shorts had taken care of that completely.

"I...I'm..." She took another deep breath, then said reasonably, "I thought this was my room."

"No," Mike said, again with the patient voice of a man with children, a man who knows how to get his point across without losing his temper, though he desperately wants to. "This is my room."

"But Mitzie," Perry began, then groaned silently to herself. She sounded like a nut. Who in their right mind takes the word of a four-year-old without asking another member of the household if that four-year-old's correct?

"Mitzie what?"

"Mitzie told me this was my room." She paused, quickly gathered her thoughts then added, "I assumed your other housekeeper used this room and that's why Mitzie knew where to put me."

"My other housekeeper lived in Vinco, with her husband. She didn't stay here."

"Oh."

"In fact, I've never had a housekeeper who wanted to stay here." He stopped, smiled, then chuckled. "Everybody was usually so darned glad to get out of here...."

He left the sentence hang as it was and though Perry understood what he was saying, the way he laughed when he said it gave her a swift rush of desire to go over and hug him. She didn't know the story about his ex-wife—Mitzie had only said her mother had left—but whatever the story, Mike McGuire had picked up the pieces, kept his kids together, made a home for them, and it looked as if he'd retained his sense of humor. That's why she wanted to hug him.

The thought of hugging him, despite her innocent intent, gave her the oddest fluttery feeling, starting at her stomach and airily gliding through her chest and lodging in her throat. She found him incredibly attractive, in a way that went beyond anything she'd ever felt for George, a man she'd come very close to marrying. What she'd felt for George was warm, loving, manageable. What she was feeling now put all her senses out of control.

But she didn't know this man, and she had no right to be attracted to him. Besides, she didn't want to be. Things were complicated enough already.

She tightened her hold on her towel. "Just tell me another room to go to and I'll be happy to leave."

He swallowed, averting his eyes. "Well, the guest room's at the other end of the hall, but . . ." He took a deep breath. "I don't think it's such a good idea for you to stay here at all."

"But I have nowhere else to go. You see, I . . ." She stopped herself before she told him she couldn't afford a hotel because that would be an out-and-out lie. She most certainly could afford a hotel. In fact, she owned two. Until now, she'd had absolutely no idea how difficult the life of a con artist was. Stretch the truth even the tiniest bit and before you know it, your whole life's a sham. And she didn't want that. The possibility still existed that she'd have to solicit this man's help to get Arthur, and the fewer lies she'd told, the easier it would be to turn to him.

She took a deep breath, clearing her thoughts again and remembered Cora telling her that sometimes the biggest reason the household staff worked as members of a household staff was for the free room and board. Obviously this guy didn't know that.

"I really thought room and board were included," she said, vowing to end the lying once and for all. She'd avoid the truth, skip the truth or tell the truth. Period.

"Well, no," he said, looking incredibly uncomfortable. And it didn't suit him. Not at all. He was meant to be confident and proud, giving orders, running the show. This stammering and stuttering was definitely out of character. He was a man of action. He was bold. Daring. Maybe even dangerous.

The attraction hit her in the stomach again and Perry unconsciously took a step backward. This was getting ridiculous. "I suppose you're right," she said, still moving toward the door backward. "Maybe it might not be such a good idea for me to stay here."

Mike felt like kicking himself. But good Lord, she was just about the most beautiful woman he'd ever seen, with her pink skin and her long, shapely legs, and he didn't want to risk another run-in like this one.

"I have an idea," he said suddenly. "I'm going to give you this room and I'll take the guest room."

"Oh, I couldn't...."

"It's no problem," Mike said, waving a dismissing hand. "The kids all sleep through the night now. I don't need to be right beside their bedrooms."

Not quite certain of how to respond, Perry tightened her hold on her towel again. "If you're sure."

"Positive," he said and just barely stopped his automatic sigh of relief. Aside from the first-floor powder room, there were two other bathrooms in this house. One was this private bath off the master bedroom, the other was the main bathroom, which wasn't isolated, as this bathroom was. Its doors opened to the hall at the top of the steps, and if he gave her any other bedroom she'd be using that bathroom. Then he'd be dealing with the scent of sweet colognes drifting into the hallway and down the steps and probably into the kitchen and halfway down the driveway. He'd see stockings, those shimmery brown stockings, hanging to dry on his shower-curtain bar, and he'd probably catch her in the hall after her bath and even if she was wearing a turtleneck robe, the glow of her pink cheeks, the smell of her bath oils, those little ringlets around her forehead would make him break out into a cold sweat.

At least until he got used to all those things again...which he would. Eventually. After all, he was a man of control.

"You take this room," he decided firmly, picked up his book and strode to the door. She shifted to accommodate his exit, but he could still smell her. "I'll see you in the morning."

He left Perry standing in the center of the room, more than a little bit confused. First it seemed as if he'd wanted to argue with her, then he'd gone out of his way to please her. But she shrugged off his odd mood, dropped her towel and went to the closet for the smooth green nightgown she'd bought at the department store.

After sliding it on, she walked to the bed, rolled back the covers, stretched out on the spot he'd just vacated, and then smelled him as acutely as if he were lying on the bed right beside her. The scent brought a quick and vivid image of his body, which brought that fluttering to her stomach again.

Oh, boy. Now she understood why he'd run out of the room.

She tossed the top two pillows to the floor and rolled the third into a ball fat enough to hold her head, albeit uncomfortably.

A complication like this one was not what she needed.

Because Mitzie told Perry her father always left the house at seven-one-five, Perry realized that though Mitzie couldn't tell time, she could read the numbers on a digital clock. Perry assumed that meant he'd be awakening about six-fifteen, which meant Perry set her alarm for six so that she could get up and have coffee ready when he came down for breakfast.

Unfortunately, when the alarm rang, Perry opened only one eye before she recognized where she was, and instead of jumping out of bed, she pulled the covers over her head.

Why in the devil hadn't she let Cora talk her out of this?

Even with the covers over her head, she heard a board creak, then another, and another, then her doorknob twisted but the door didn't open. Still, Perry didn't waste a second wondering who was at her door and why. After last night, she knew precautions came before thought.

She bounced out of bed and grabbed her green, rust and black paisley robe. The knob twisted again, but this time the door opened and Mitzie entered, her arms stretched their full distance to reach the doorknob, her scraggly bear in her teeth.

Perry stooped to Mitzie's height and whispered, "Mitzie, what are you doing up this early?"

Mitzie took her bear from her mouth, walked over to Perry and attached herself, wrapping one arm around Perry's neck and one leg around her back. If Perry hadn't caught her, Mitzie would have slid off Perry's shimmery paisley robe.

"I missed you."

"Missed me?" Perry said, then she frowned. "But..." The second the word was out of her mouth, Perry understood, or thought she might understand what Mitzie was trying to say. She hadn't missed Perry, it was more like she was checking to make sure Perry was still here. She also sensed this was not something of which to make an issue. "Okay, well, what would you like for breakfast?"

Grinning, Mitzie said, "Pancakes."

"Pancakes!" Perry gasped, then tickled Mitzie's warm belly. "You know I can't cook. Don't you dare even say the word 'pancake' when we get down into the kitchen."

"No. I want a pancake," Mitzie insisted and giggled with glee.

Perry laughed, hoisting Mitzie to her hip as she rose. "At this point, a wise little girl would get a sudden craving for cornflakes."

"How about Cocoa Critters?"

"Cocoa Critters will do nicely," Perry agreed, opened the door and began walking down the hall. When they reached the kitchen, Mitzie turned on the light switch. After the click of the light, the soft swishing sound of Perry's satin night-gown and paisley robe were the only sounds in the room. Mitzie seemed content to hold her bear and cling to Perry, and Perry found she could actually fill a filter with coffee grounds, pour water into the coffeemaker and hit the switch while she carried a cuddling four-year-old.

"Coffee ready yet?" Mike entered the kitchen talking, but stopped short when he saw a sight that hit him directly in the stomach. Mitzie was wrapped around a sleep-disheveled woman and that woman was dressed in the most incredibly soft-looking robe and nightgown. He could almost feel the shimmering satin brushing against his skin as he slid into bed, or in those last few seconds before he nodded off to sleep, or even better, when he first awakened, when his senses were heightened. When making love happened as naturally as breathing. . . .

Good Lord, he had to get out of here.

He cleared his throat. "Well, I can see the coffee's only beginning to run through, so I think I'll just grab a cup at Sheetz." He paused, noting that both his housekeeper and his baby girl were looking at him as if he were crazy. After a quick breath, he began to stroll into the room and said, "I'm a little behind at work. If the coffee was ready, I would have poured some into a thermal cup, but since it's not, I'll leave now. . . ."

He walked directly into a chair and destroyed his shin but kept right on talking and smiling. He didn't even flinch. "To go to Sheetz, so I can catch up on that extra paperwork."

Mitzie stuck her thumb in her mouth. His housekeeper didn't say anything, then both spoke at once. Perry politely let Mitzie talk first.

"Do I get a kiss, Dad?"

"Sure, Pumpkin," Mike replied automatically, then saw Mitzie wasn't moving. She was wrapped around Perry's slim neck and tiny waist and she was staying there. For thirty seconds of insanity, Mike understood completely and most certainly didn't blame his daughter.

But he regained his sanity and said, "Jump down, hon, and Daddy will give you a hug and a kiss."

Mitzie sniffed and nuzzled into Perry's neck. "You come here."

Mike frowned. The very last thing in the world he needed right now was to go over and stick his nose into the housekeeper's neck in order to kiss Mitzie. And that's what he'd be doing, if Mitzie continued to refuse. Which was also out of character. Mitzie might not always obey her sitter, but she never argued with her dad. If he didn't know better, he'd think Mitzie was doing all this on purpose. Hunkering down to Mitzie's height, he said, "No, Mitzie, you come here."

Mitzie slid down Perry's side and scampered over as if absolutely nothing unusual had happened. In the last second before she reached her father, she pulled her thumb out of her mouth. When she threw her arms around him, she slapped his back with her bear and when she kissed him, she gave him the same sloppy smack she always did.

Confused, Mike rose, then said, "I'll see you around six," and walked out of the kitchen. He had the oddest sensation that he'd just totally and completely lost control of his world.

Perry, on the other hand, felt herself gain a little bit of control. She didn't have to taste the coffee to know it was as strong as two sumo wrestlers and she was awfully darned glad Mike McGuire hadn't taken a cup. Lifting the scoop she'd used to measure, Perry sighed. The little handle said "one cup" and she put in one cup of coffee grinds for every cup of liquid coffee she expected to get. So why'd it turn out looking like mud?

She shook her head. After she poured Mitzie a bowl of Cocoa Critters, she guessed she'd better call Cora.

Chapter Six

Mike snuck onto his driveway that night after work, his heart thumping and his palms as sweaty as two ditchdiggers in August. Even from the road, he could see the bikes belonging to the boys standing in a neat row beside the garage and the light in the kitchen window.

Everybody was home. Everybody was probably waiting for him. And he'd deliberately worked overtime. His car rolled to a stop just inside the garage doors and he twisted the key to silence the ignition. After taking a deep breath, he pushed open the door, bounded out and headed for the door to the house.

Immediately upon entry, he realized that the kitchen light was the only light burning. The rest of the house was pitch-dark and quiet. He drew another deep breath, his heart pounding out a slow, steady rhythm and his knees turning to rubber. He knew exactly what was going on here. The boys had become attached to this woman as quickly as Mitzie had. And they were sharing the same room with her.

Maybe playing a game. Maybe doing homework. Maybe even helping her do the dishes.

They were pitiful. All of them. Each and every one of them was so starved for female attention that in one short day they'd become enamored with this woman as if she were a saint, or something.

But he was the worst. Thinking of her in his office that afternoon, Mike had decided that his desperation had probably led him to attribute characteristics to his housekeeper that she really didn't have. She couldn't be as pretty as he'd remembered. She couldn't be as sweet as he'd remembered. Hell, she probably didn't even smell half as nice or feel one-fourth as soft as he'd fantasized. And now, now was the moment of truth. Eyes open and fantasies squelched, he'd see her as she really was.

He made his way down the hall and pushed open the kitchen door.

"Hi."

Everyone looked up at him. Seated on either side of Perry, Timmy and Tommy appeared to be knee-deep in homework. Across the table, Mitzie was making a masterpiece with a fat crayon and the back of an old cardboard box.

Mitzie yelled, "Dad!" and the twins shot off their chairs and ran to hug him. But even as the boys hooked themselves to his thighs, Mike felt his mouth go dry.

Well, he hadn't imagined the incredible beauty of her strawberry-blond locks. And neither had he exaggerated the delicate features of her face. Her peachy skin glowed even in the harsh light of the kitchen and her round brown eyes held the same deep, rich color as freshly brewed coffee.

No. He hadn't imagined anything.

Ruffling Timmy's hair, Mike cleared his throat. "Sorry I was late, but I had to read some articles."

Perry smiled at him as she rose from her chair. "Would you like me to heat up your dinner?"

She wore another ugly sweat suit, the kind a person bought at a discount store and used only for terrible jobs like cleaning the garage or scrubbing a really filthy house, but somehow or other, her body seemed to make the formless, wretched-looking gray garment come to life. Her round hips gave the elastic-waist pants a nice, soft fullness and the tips of her breasts neatly angled the baggy top.

Mike shook his head. If he didn't soon force himself to grow accustomed to seeing her, to dealing with her attractiveness and her femininity, he was not only going to lose his baby-sitter, he'd probably lose his mind.

"No. It's late. I think I'll just take this one upstairs," he said as he reached out to pull Mitzie off her seat, "and give her her bath. She looks about ready to nod off."

Mitzie smiled at him and sleepily nestled into his neck.

"That's okay," Perry said. Arms extended, she prepared to coax Mitzie from him. "I'll be happy to bathe her. You sit down. Eat a hamburger."

"No," Mike insisted and turned toward the door. He'd learned a very valuable lesson when he decided to quit smoking. He had eliminated one cigarette at a time. The process took him about a year before he'd completely quit, but the point was he had quit. And it wasn't a hardship, it was easy. So, to grow accustomed to the baby-sitter, he'd just reverse the process. He'd adjust to her, bring her into his life, one step at a time. Tonight, he'd survived arriving home and greeting her. Tomorrow morning, he'd tackle breakfast. Tomorrow night, he'd deal with dinner. By the end of the week, they'd be watching TV together.

For tonight, he'd already managed as much as he could handle without tripping over something, saying something stupid or accidentally staring at her in an inappropriate, obvious way.

"I always help the kids get ready for bed. I want to make
sure I take care of Mitzie before she falls asleep. Besides, I'm
not hungry." With that, he left the kitchen, walked back to
the hall and began a slow ascent toward the second-floor
bathroom.

There, see, he told himself as he climbed the steps. *That
wasn't so bad. In fact, that was downright normal.* And,
dammit, he had to be normal. Otherwise, he'd never convince this woman his mother had been wrong—that he
didn't want a wife, only a housekeeper.

It was eight-thirty before the boys' homework was completed, and the minute the last answer to the last math
problem was written on the last line of each of their papers,
Perry snapped the book closed and rose from the table.

"Well, boys," she said, smiling at both of them as they
grinned at her. "I think I'm going to sneak up the back
stairs and go to bed."

"Aren't you gonna watch TV?" Timmy asked incredulously.

"Actually," Perry admitted honestly, "I don't watch a
whole heck of a lot of TV. Cora always said it was better to
read." With that comment, Perry turned both boys away
from her and pointed them in the direction of the front hall.
"That's why I think you should go upstairs, get your baths,
find your father and suggest he help you choose a book to
read tonight, instead."

"Dad would have a heart attack and then die," Tommy
said, stretching his neck back to look upside down at Perry.

She winked at him. "Let's risk it."

After her shower, Perry peeked out into the hall, and
though all the lights were out, she heard the faint sounds of
music and voices, an indication that the TV was indeed on.
It was after nine, so she doubted the children were watching. That meant that if she ventured downstairs to wish her

employer good-night, they'd be alone. No kids. No three-foot-tall bodyguards.

She glanced down at her paisley robe. It was perfectly covering, but given the fact that it was a robe and beneath it was a thin nightgown, which covered a newly scrubbed body, Perry had serious second thoughts. Part of her was absolutely certain a man with three children would have accurately read her reaction to him last night. Not more than three minutes had gone by today when she didn't get a flashback of his hair-covered body or those silky red boxer shorts. He was a very sexy man and they were the only two adults in this house. A woman who said good-night to a man while wearing a robe wasn't merely asking for trouble, she could be considered to be issuing an invitation.

Perry closed the bedroom door, slowly making her way to the bed. No. They didn't need any more crossed wires. From here on out, everything would have to be carefully and thoroughly thought through. There would be no more mistakes for Perry Pierson.

That's why she dressed completely the minute she got out of bed the next morning. Even though she recognized Mitzie's tap at the door, she didn't invite the little girl into the bedroom until her sweatpants were in place and her sweatshirt was secured, just in case the man of the house was walking down the hall or standing at such an angle that he could see into her room.

Totally clothed, Perry opened her door and immediately looked down. Mitzie stood before her, bear over the crook of her arm, blanket around her neck and thumb in her mouth.

"Good morning," Perry said, bending to bring Mitzie into her arms.

"Are we gonna have eggs?" Mitzie asked, but she whispered. In only a little over forty-eight hours, Mitzie understood the rules of this game very well—as well, it seemed, as she understood that unless she kept the rules and didn't accidentally leak any confidential information, Perry would probably be fired.

"That's why Perry spent two hours on the phone with Aunt Cora yesterday. To learn how to make those eggs."

"Am I gonna make the toast?"

Perry grimaced. "I think you're going to have to. I don't think I'm good enough to make two things at once yet."

They walked down the hall full of confidence, but before they reached the top of the back stairs, Perry smelled coffee brewing and her spirits sank to her feet. "Uh-oh, we're late."

Mitzie said, "Huh?" and, thinking quickly, as she had become accustomed to doing, Perry shook her head. "Never mind. We'll just go downstairs and ask your father if he wants eggs. If he does, we'll pretend we're playing a game and that's why you're making toast. Understand?"

Mitzie happily nodded and Perry took a long breath. Tomorrow, she'd set her alarm for five-thirty.

The back steps led directly to the kitchen, and as Perry descended them, she smelled the bacon. Bacon. Real food. She breathed in the scent appreciatively. If he hadn't made enough for five people, it wasn't going to be easy to pretend she didn't want any of that.

"Good morning," she said, taking the last step into the kitchen. Mike stood by the stove, wearing an emerald green terry cloth robe over his dress shirt and pants and holding a spatula. At least two pounds of bacon drained on paper towels and the aroma that filled the room sent her taste buds into ecstasy. She'd been eating frozen food for only two days, but to Perry's tongue it felt like a lifetime.

"Morning," he said, but he didn't look at her. His attention seemed to be totally taken by his cooking.

As Perry slid Mitzie onto her chair, she leaned her head to the left so that her hair would create a sort of cover and glanced over at him through her curls. Any other man who put a robe over his dress clothes would look utterly ridiculous. Somehow, Mike McGuire managed to make even that look sexy. And there was a part of her, a part that she really hadn't known existed, that took an extra minute settling Mitzie so she could enjoy that minute looking at him. It was the kind of extravagance she couldn't indulge in Boston where the entire population knew who she was and half of them watched her as if she were royalty. But here in this wonderful little town where no one knew who she was and nobody as much as gave her a second glance, Perry could do anything she wanted.

So, she took advantage of that minute to indulge in the simple pleasure of really looking at a handsome man. She took in the crisp pleat of his gray trousers, the shine on his black shoes, the very sexy way his robe rounded his buttocks and smoothed up his back, the terribly masculine hairs that peppered his forearms, and the black shadow of his beard, even though his face was newly shaved.

Until she'd come here, she'd had absolutely no idea of all the things she'd missed. She wasn't angry that she'd been deprived of some wonderful simple pleasures, she wasn't jealous of the people who had them, she was deliciously curious. Being at home alone all day with a wonderful little girl and absolutely no pressure, save that of learning how to do menial tasks, Perry found herself peaceful and content for the first time in her whole life. It was a bonus she hadn't expected, but one she planned to exploit while she could. She'd always wondered how the other half lived and now she was experiencing it.

Straightening away from Mitzie, Perry hid her smile. If she would have known this kind of life was so much fun, she would have done this years ago.

"Did you sleep well?" she asked, fully enjoying this newfound freedom. As she spoke, she walked to the cupboard for some plates.

"Yes," Mike answered, but his response was quick, almost strained, and Perry pivoted to face him. She was so caught up in the excitement of being able to indulge in a few simple pleasures that she never even thought to realize that her employer might not appreciate having to make his own breakfast. And his short temper might, in fact, be an indicator that he was waiting for her to volunteer to finish making the bacon.

And she didn't know how!

For thirty seconds, Perry stood rooted to the spot while Mike retrieved the last strips of bacon from the black skillet and set them on a clean paper towel. With a quick flip of his wrist, he turned off the burner and Perry whirled to face the cupboard.

When he spun away from the stove, Mike was fully prepared to see the mass of strawberry-blond hair that spilled over her shoulders and down her back. He was even prepared for the impact it would have on his psyche and his breathing. Nonetheless, seeing her, actually physically seeing her, sent feelings and needs through him the likes of which Mike was absolutely positive should be illegal.

No matter how much he wanted nothing more than an employer-employee relationship with this woman, or how hard he tried to bring her into his life one encounter at a time, he couldn't seem to get acclimatized to her, and he had to admit his mother had done the ultimate. She'd found a woman to whom Mike was attracted, genuinely, uncontrollably physically attracted. Despite the fact that Mike didn't want to be attracted to anyone, this woman was driving him crazy. He was nervous, sweaty and he couldn't seem to breathe right.

He dropped the bacon to the kitchen table. "Good morning, Mitzie," he said, then cleared his throat because his voice sounded high and squeaky. His pulse pounded in his throat and his breathing felt like hot lava as it entered air-starved lungs. After years and years of unquestioned control, it was hard to believe his body was betraying him this way.

"I wanted to surprise the kids with breakfast," he said, looking down at the belt of his robe as he untied it. "But it looks like I only had time to make the bacon. Would you mind making her a scrambled egg?"

"No! Perry loves to make eggs!" Mitzie cried, her eyes wide with excitement, her pert little mouth bowing upward into a delighted smile. "And I can make the toast."

"Whatever," Mike said, turning toward the back stairway. In the last second before he would have begun his ascent, he changed his mind and pivoted toward Mitzie. In two quick strides, he was beside her. He bent, kissed the top of her head and said, "Sorry, Pumpkin, but Dad's gotta run. I won't be back down this way, I'm just going to head on out to the car."

With that, he was off. He whirled around, took the area between himself and the steps in two long strides, then raced up the steps.

Perry stood staring at the stairway. The blood that flowed through her veins felt like ice water. The only possible explanation for his quick getaway was that he'd seen the way she was staring at him—gawking at him—and she'd embarrassed not only herself but him, as well.

The man was going to fire her.

And she wouldn't blame him.

Not one darned bit.

She couldn't cook, couldn't clean and stared at him as if she had a right to. If their situations were reversed, Perry would fire him in a minute.

So, now it had to be war. Before he realized she wasn't a housekeeper, baby-sitter or even a normal person, Perry had to get him to open up to her about Arthur, and if that meant pulling out a few stops, then so be it.

Chapter Seven

Mike slid into the front door of his home, taking great pains not to make a sound. Quietly, he pushed the heavy wooden portal closed, then turned and began tiptoeing up the stairway.

Luck was with him and not one board creaked, and then suddenly, like the blare of trumpets, Mitzie's voice announced, "Hey, Perry, Dad's home."

The child was destined to be a reporter.

Sighing, he glanced down the open stairway at his grinning four-year-old. "Tell Perry your dad's going upstairs to change before dinner," he told his daughter, then continued his ascent, this time not caring about his noise level.

In his temporary bedroom, he stripped off his suit jacket and sat on the bed to remove his shoes. He couldn't believe what was happening to him, but all he had to do was look around this tiny, ruffly, far too feminine bedroom to be reminded that the woman in his kitchen had arrived here five days ago and had managed to turn his entire world upside down.

That's why he was in his bedroom instead of in the kitchen. Every night, he took ten minutes to compose himself. Ten minutes to get himself ready for the scent of her cologne, to brace himself for the sight of her shiny strawberry-blond hair and to remind himself that no matter how wonderful it would be to talk with the articulate, intelligent woman who took such great care of his children, he had to keep his mouth shut. But, even more important, he took ten minutes to focus on the fact that his mother hadn't called once, not even once since Monday, not to ask about the kids, not to ask about the business, not to see if the housekeeper was working out.

The only reason Mike could think of that his mother wouldn't call was that she didn't want to risk questions. And if she didn't want to risk questions, it could only be because she didn't have good answers. Or else, she was deliberately trying to give them tons and tons of time alone, time to be a family, time to fall in love. If that wasn't proof positive that there was more to his mother's hiring this woman than his need for a housekeeper, nothing was.

Yet, despite the fact that he knew exactly what was going on, and that he'd been virtually living with Perry for almost a week, he still couldn't stop his heart from pounding when she got too close, or his breath from catching when she smiled at him, or his fingers from itching to touch her.

It was insanity.

He removed his trousers, then pulled on a pair of jeans and a soft green sweater. He couldn't believe how easy it was to forget that Perry had probably been handpicked by his mother to be her new daughter-in-law, not his housekeeper. But he knew why it was so easy to forget that. Perry was soft-spoken, she was sweet, she was dedicated. She was good with the kids, very easy on the eyes, and if it wasn't for the fact that her scent seemed to linger, Mike really wouldn't know she was around a lot of the time. She was nothing like the women his mother usually chose for him, but that made him all the more suspicious. After three years of trial and error, Mary McGuire seemed to have found the right combination of attributes a woman would need to drive her son completely crazy.

He took a deep breath, fortified now to go downstairs and help Perry finish the dinner preparations. This really was not impossible. After all, they'd been doing it for five days. And surely, he'd get used to her eventually.

In the hall, he took one final deep breath and then pushed open the swinging door to the kitchen, but instead of seeing a kitchen table loaded with dishes and food, there were only two places set. A small casserole that looked like lasagna sat in the middle of the table and beside it was a bottle of white wine. In the center of the table sat a huge bouquet of flowers.

"What are you doing?" he said, but the last word sort of dropped out of his mouth because she straightened away from the table and Mike saw her dress. His first thought wasn't why the hell was she dressed so elegantly. His first and only thought was that the dress was gorgeous, but Perry was even more beautiful.

The bright red dress was cut simply and actually looked like something Jennifer, his top salesperson, would wear for a lunch meeting, but Perry's figure and her exquisite good looks wouldn't allow any outfit to be plain. Even the simple gold jewelry she wore—shiny chains around her neck, around her wrist and hanging from her ears—took on an elegant, luxurious glow next to her skin. Her hair had been pulled to the top of her head, like a curly mop, but it wasn't tight or too controlled, it was loose. Loose, fluffy, curly. Beautiful in a sort of haphazard way.

Oh, boy. He was in trouble.

He took a jagged breath, licked his dry lips and croaked, "Are we expecting company?"

Smiling brightly, Perry looked up at him. "Actually, no. The boys begged to stay with the Coopers overnight, since tomorrow's Saturday and they don't have school. And when I checked on Mitzie a minute ago, I found her asleep in her room. So, it's just going to be the two of us tonight."

And it was. She'd spent five days in this house trying to get that man to say more than a two-word sentence to her and she'd failed miserably. So, she'd purchased lasagna from a restaurant, wine from a liquor store and flowers from a florist. Then, she'd found an unpretentious negotiating dress, understated gold jewelry and had her hair done the way she wore it for every business dinner she'd attended for the past six years.

She'd feed him, get him mellow with wine and then pry out every darned tidbit of information about Arthur's takeover that she could.

"Have a seat."

With only one foot in the door, Mike stood frozen, caught between a confrontation about his mother, and the very real truth that he couldn't risk losing not just the best baby-sitter he'd ever had but the only baby-sitter he'd been able to find in a month. Despite the odd and awkward circumstances every night when he arrived home, he had to admit that his days were free of worry about Mitzie and the boys. If he confronted Perry, she would probably quit—that is, if he didn't take the argument so far, he ended up firing her.

Common sense dictated that he needed a baby-sitter more than he needed the satisfaction of getting her to admit she was in league with his mother. But common sense also told him that having a private dinner with her would be something like singing on the way to the gas chamber.

"Uh, I hadn't planned on...well, you see I...I... I wanted to catch the news tonight," he said, almost sighing with relief that he'd thought of a way to get out of the room.

"Oh," Perry said, and though she looked nonplussed for a second or two, she recovered so quickly, Mike didn't see it coming. "That's a great idea. I'd like to see the news, myself."

"Well, you know, you don't have to," Mike said, walking to the table as if nothing were wrong, though his palms had started to sweat and he was definitely having trouble breathing. Come hell or high water, he had to get out of this, but it had to be gracefully. He picked up a plate and scooped out one of the precut portions of lasagna with the spatula sitting beside the tin casserole dish. "I mean, you haven't had a minute to yourself in the five days you've been here. Why don't you just take the night off? I'll wash the dishes."

She smiled brightly. "No. Don't be silly. You hired a housekeeper so you wouldn't have to do dishes. I'm not going to let you wash them tonight."

She also wasn't going to let him eat alone, Mike quickly realized when she picked up the second plate and served herself a helping of dinner. Though he didn't wait for her, or offer any politeness or kindness at all, he didn't have to look behind him to know Perry followed him into the living room. He sat on the couch to take advantage of using the coffee table as a resting place for his plate, and as if playing a game of follow the leader, Perry took the seat right beside him, setting her plate next to his and smiling at him when she saw he was watching her.

He tugged at the collar of his sweater. "Is it hot in here?"

"No," Perry said, but she laughed. "You just came in out of the cold, that's why it feels warm to you."

"Yeah. Yeah, I guess that's it," Mike agreed as he surreptitiously slid his plate a little farther from Perry's, and slid himself a little farther down the couch cushion. "It's pretty darned cold out there."

"Yes, it is," Perry said, smiling as she nodded her agreement.

"Coldest September I remember," Mike said, wondering what the hell he'd say next. Or if he even should say anything. Maybe he should just ignore her. Maybe if he would ignore her—everything she said, all those little movements of hers on the couch—maybe she'd get the hint and leave.

Perry couldn't help but notice that Mike was incredibly nervous and that caused her to remember she'd forgotten the wine she'd bought to make him mellow. "I'll be right back," she said, rising from the couch. "There's no sense in chilling wine if you're not going to drink it."

"Well, Perry, actually, I'm not much in the mood for wine," Mike said, then almost bit his tongue. It wouldn't be such a bad idea to have the few minutes she spent retrieving the bottle and the glasses to compose himself. In fact, if she were gone long enough, he might be able to pull himself together enough that he could ignore her when she returned. "But since it's here and chilled, why not?"

She looked down at him and bestowed upon him the most beautiful, most angelic smile Mike had ever seen, and when she finally slid through the door and into the kitchen, he fell back on the cushions and breathed a long sigh of relief. If he didn't soon think of a way to get himself under control around this woman, he'd either end up married to the woman of his mother's choice, or he'd lose the only babysitter he could find. Neither prospect thrilled him, and actually both brought him to his senses somewhat. He took a long breath, sat up on the couch and vowed, absolutely vowed, that even if it killed him, he wouldn't let her use this intimate setting to start something. The tough part would be finding a way to halt her conversational efforts without making himself look like an ogre or an idiot and without insulting her to the point that she left. He had to keep this strictly professional.

Perry returned carrying two long-stemmed glasses and a wine bottle wrapped in a dishcloth. Mike lifted a forkful of lasagna to his lips, and as he did so, the strangest thing happened. Perry's mind seemed to home in and concentrate on his mouth, the way his full lips wrapped around the food. She watched his fork go down to the lasagna again, watched his forearm flex as he cut another bite, then watched him as he lifted the fork again. Only this time, her attention wasn't drawn by only his mouth, but by all of him. He sat forward on the couch, causing his thighs to pull the material of his worn jeans to their limit. His sweater hugged his broad chest like a comfortable second skin. Black hair peppered the backs of his hands in a very attractive, very masculine way. He was so different from her. Where she was round, he was angled. She was small, he was big. She was feminine, he was definitely one-hundred-percent grade-A male.

It wasn't until he pulled the fork away from his mouth with a satisfied groan that Perry came back to reality and realized she was blatantly staring at him. Not only that but her breathing had gone shallow and her legs felt weak and rubbery.

"This is wonderful," he said, unable to stop the comment or another groan of pleasure that naturally followed it.

"Thanks," she said, a little nervous about accepting a compliment for something she didn't make, but even more nervous about something she hadn't counted on. She found this man attractive. He found her attractive. They were alone, on a couch, about to have wine. And unless she got herself under control, all the plans she'd made and spent the afternoon and several hundred dollars bringing to fruition would be for nothing.

"Mr. McGuire," she began uncertainly.

He glanced over. "Yes."

"Well, you know, I was thinking this afternoon that even though I've been here for five days, there are a lot of things you and I haven't discussed or decided."

Mike sat back on the couch. He crossed his legs, put one arm along the back cushions and gave her his full attention. "Such as?"

Despite the fact that Mike McGuire was offering a very sexy, very masculine pose, his demeanor came across as being incredibly defensive, causing Perry to rethink her strategy. Because there really were many things about which they'd never spoken, including but not limited to her salary, her days off and any restrictions Mitzie or the twins might have, she didn't think this discussion would strike him as odd or unusual. In fact, that's why she'd chosen to open the conversation this way. But since he didn't appear to be too thrilled with this line of discussion and since she didn't want him defensive, but cooperative, she took a deep breath and tried a more optimistic approach. "You know, you're such a good father...."

He cocked an eyebrow. "That surprises you?"

"No! Oh, no! It's just that most fathers don't have the opportunity to, you know, spend as much time with their kids as you've spent over the last few days...especially doing things like helping me with dinner, and I just wondered if you could tell me a little bit about what you do at the newspaper office."

"Do?"

"Do for a living that allows you to be home every night."

"Perry, most men come home for dinner every night."

"Well, my dad didn't. He owned his own business and made a commitment to build that business," she said honestly, trying to keep the comment as truthful, yet generic, as possible, because she knew the best way to get people to talk about themselves was to tell them a little bit about herself first. The trick to this would be telling him just enough that he'd respond to her remark with a statement about his life, then continue to get him to expand on that observation so that they wouldn't get back on the subject of her life again. "So, when he wasn't working long hours, he was traveling."

"Really," Mike said, glancing over at her again. He hadn't intended to get into a conversation with her, but he wasn't so foolish as to throw away this opportunity to get to know her better. If they talked long enough, she might just say something that would help Mike find her unattractive. Beauty really was only skin-deep, and Mike had to admit that up to this point, his overall reaction to her wasn't anything more than physical. The trick to this would be telling her just enough to answer her question, then segue the conversation to her life again.

"I didn't have a whole lot of choice in the matter. I'm a single parent, I have to be home for my children, so I am. I honestly feel that if you look hard enough, you can find a way to manage your schedule to give you time for your family. I guess that's why I'm curious about what kind of a business would be so important or difficult that it could keep a father away long hours like that. What kind of business does your father own?"

"Well, he owns several," Perry said quietly, absently setting the wineglasses on the coffee table. "Some out of town," she added after a few seconds of deliberation. Thinking on her feet had always come easy for Perry, and even the way Mike had bounced the conversation back to her like a tennis ball at Wimbledon, hadn't thrown her concentration, or confused her. Though it did cause her to wonder if he hadn't done it deliberately. "And it's probably that difference that gives you options my father didn't have."

"I think that's a matter of perspective," Mike said, then glanced at the wine. She hadn't made a move to fill the glasses and she was nervous, not really hedging the conversation, but definitely choosing her words with care. Without a second's hesitation, he reached for the wine bottle and the glasses. They were into this, too far into this, to stop now. In order to keep her as a baby-sitter, he'd have to like and trust her as a person. In order to be able to like and trust her as a person, he'd have to find a way to diminish her attractiveness. Her nervousness really made him feel she was hiding enough of a secret or a past to make *even her* unattractive. And, it was for both of their own good that Mike popped the cork on the wine, filled both glasses and decided they'd see this thing through to the end.

"So, Perry," he said, handing her a glass of wine, "tell me more about your dad and his companies. I'm curious."

The very last topic of conversation Perry wished to share with Mike McGuire was her father. In fact, she wasn't really sure how this conversation kept going askew, but she wasn't going to let it go the whole way to Hades in a hand basket, and the way she had it figured, she could clear this whole mess up in about three sentences, then get back to the business at hand. "My dad is a wonderful man who became incredibly successful. Despite the fact that we really didn't spend much time together when I was a child, we made up for it eventually. That's why it strikes me as being good that you spend time with your children now."

"Was it a difficult reconciliation?" Mike asked, then leaned forward to give her his full attention.

"There wasn't a reconciliation," Perry said, laughing slightly as if to prove to him that he was on the wrong track.

"You still have your differences, then?"

"No," Perry assured, glancing over at him. "My dad and I get along wonderfully."

"Gee, that's funny. I'd never guess that from the way you get so nervous when you talk about him."

"I am not nervous," Perry said, then burst from the couch and began to pace. "It's just that I'm trying to talk about my job, and my dad has nothing to do with my working here." Even as she said the last, Perry got a strange blush because she was lying. Her dad *was* the reason she was sitting in this farmhouse, pretending she was a housekeeper, trying to get poor Mike McGuire to spill his guts about his business. If she really had a good relationship with her father, if her father trusted her as much as he trusted Arthur, she wouldn't be here now.

That piece of knowledge was so profound and so bitterly true, she felt something like a wave of nausea roll over her, and she couldn't think. Her brain almost seemed to come to a crashing halt. And without the ability to think quickly, she was absolutely no match for the man sprawled on the couch. In fact, even with her brain functioning well, she would have to admit he'd just bested her.

She drew in a long breath. "Look, I don't want to talk about my father. Okay? And, if it's all right with you, I think I might just take you up on your offer to do the dishes."

With that, she turned to leave the living room, but Mike sprang from the couch and caught her arm before she'd even taken a step. "Hey, I'm sorry," he said, grasping her by the shoulders and turning her to face him. "I'm not really sure how we got into that conversation, but I didn't mean to upset you. I apologize, because I got carried away."

Perry couldn't look at him. She didn't want to face him. She was so thunderstruck by the realization that it had taken a perfect stranger to make her see her own father didn't trust her, that she wanted nothing more than some time alone to try to come to terms with it. She'd been working for her father for six years. When her father retired, complete control of Omnipotence would be hers. Yet, he didn't trust her. It wasn't a question of finding evidence to prove Arthur was corrupt. The truth of the matter was, she should be able to go to her father with her suspicions and have him listen, not question. And she knew very well she couldn't do that.

"Hey," Mike said again, this time lifting her chin with his index finger. "I am really sorry."

Perry sort of laughed. "Don't be. You probably did me a favor."

"You don't look like a woman who just received a favor."

"Trust me," Perry said, straightening her spine and smiling at the man who still held her biceps in his strong hands and who bestowed upon her a soft, understanding smile. "I'll be fine."

"Yeah," Mike said, "I think you will, but you see, I'm not quite so sure I will."

Her eyes were slightly bright, an indication that despite the fact that she'd force herself to be strong, she was indeed vulnerable, and that combination had a very potent appeal. Life might not have dealt her the perfect hand, but Mike could see in her expression that Perry didn't complain about her cards, she simply learned how to play them. With that knowledge came the understanding of why he found her so attractive. She wasn't merely kind and smart, she was wise. Kind to his children. Smart enough to figure out answers when problems arose. Wise about life. And unbelievably beautiful. It was no wonder he found her nearly irresistible.

"Oh, come on," Perry scoffed. "You look like a real scrapper to me. I can't imagine anything you can't handle."

"How about this?" Mike asked, then bent his head and kissed her.

For Perry, the effect was something like magic. Physical attraction manifested itself instantly and would have been overwhelming, save that it was tempered by something more powerful, something more compelling. Understanding. And compassion. Which somehow fed passion.

She didn't merely feel the smooth velvet caresses of his mouth. The airy brush of his lips across hers was a silent articulation of his yet unspoken feelings, a physical whisper of genuine affection for her. In one short conversation, they'd formed a bond that transformed lust into desire. Real desire. Not a mere physical need but rather a gentle yearning inspired by deep emotions. A yearning so strong, it compelled them forward, yet so delicate, they hovered on the precipice, unwilling to go any farther, kiss any deeper, for fear of damaging something priceless, something precious.

The experience was unique, unparalleled. No one had ever treated Perry so gently, so genuinely. Everybody thought of her as Graham Pierson's daughter, a woman half pursued for money, half pursued for fame. No one ever sought her for her. But here was a man who liked her, really liked her, because of things she'd said and done, not because of her father, not because of her background.

She lifted her arms and wrapped them around Mike's broad shoulders, seeking both the physical touch and strength of him, as well as the acceptance. He hardly knew her, but his kiss was an indicator that he'd take her as she was and she clung to him, pressed her mouth against his hungrily and then opened her lips upon his urging.

"Hey! Did you guys forget about me!"

The sound of Mitzie's voice blowing into the room didn't merely interrupt the mood, it broke them apart like two guilty teenagers. Perry's heart pounded in her chest, her lips were moist and dewy from soft kisses, but her unsteady legs held her up just enough to turn and face the four-year-old standing in the doorway, angrily clutching her bear.

Mike seemed to recover without any effort at all. "No, honey," he said, completely ignoring the obvious. "Are you hungry?"

"Yes!" she said grumpily.

"Then Daddy will get you some food."

"I want Perry to!" Mitzie demanded testily.

"Well, you're getting your daddy because Perry's tired." With that, he turned and scooped Mitzie into his arms. "Good night, Perry," he said, then left the room without another word.

Chapter Eight

"**I**'ve never been more confused in my entire life."

Mike sat in his office, behind the huge oak desk, which had been handcrafted by his grandfather. The venetian blinds that covered the window to the newsroom were pulled tight.

He didn't have a big paper. In fact, he thought he probably owned the smallest newspaper in the world, and he couldn't believe some huge conglomerate wanted his territory, even though he did get great money for advertising from the stores in Johnstown. But now that their interest seemed to have finally cooled and Omnipotence hadn't made their usual weekly job offer, he had to deal with his mother's conspiracy.

Sam looked at him quizzically. "Why?"

"I would bet the paper on the fact that my mother hired this woman so we'd fall in love."

"And?"

"And, normally, just knowing that would be enough to turn me off, but instead, I find her ureasonably appealing."

Sam started to laugh. "I think you're making things worse by being so nervous."

Mike and Sam had been classmates, they'd graduated together from Central Cambria High School. Mike had gone on to college, Sam into the coal mines and eventually he'd become a union representative. For a while it looked as if Sam had really made it, then the mines began to close and Sam lost his job, just when Mike realized he'd need a little help managing the paper, especially the paper's employees. Neither had ever been sorry they'd made the partnership.

Mike rose, paced to the window and said, "Do you think I don't know that?"

"Then just relax."

"I can't. Having her around is driving me absolutely crazy."

Sam frowned, considering the situation, then said, "Mike, she's the first baby-sitter you've ever hired who can handle Mitzie. Why don't you just ignore her?"

"Because I'm not sure I should do that." Mike paused, embarrassed, then took a deep breath and said, "My God, Sam, she's beautiful, the twins think she's great, Mitzie instantly loved her, and she insisted on living with us—and let's not forget she was coincidentally planted in my bedroom."

Sam grinned, then laughed outright. "That Mitzie's a character."

"That Mitzie might be in on this."

"I think you're worrying about nothing," Sam said, hiding another grin by studying his fingernails. "So, what are you going to do? Call your mother and yell at her for sending you a woman you find irresistible?"

"No, I know I can't do that. It'll only make matters worse. I'd have to acknowledge that I find Perry attractive—and that would thrill my mother to death. Besides, she'd never admit she'd done it and I'd end up looking like an idiot," Mike said, then sank into his thick chair again. He braced his hands on both of the chair's arms, put his head back and closed his eyes.

Sam blew his breath out on a long sigh. "To me, that's all the more reason you should just relax with this baby-sitter. She's taking better care of Mitzie than Mrs. Martin ever did. She's literally taking the bulk of your troubles off your shoulders and freeing you to be focused when you're here. And, Mike, sooner or later, you're bound to get used to having her around."

Mike groaned. "Fat chance."

Sam grinned. "Uh-oh," he said, chuckling knowingly. "You're not telling me everything." He paused, waiting for Mike to elaborate, and when he didn't, Sam laughed heartily. "Something really juicy happened, didn't it?"

"Good news."

Perry had hardly said, "Hello," before Cora started chatting excitedly.

"There's a strike in Argentina and your father sent Arthur down to settle things. Arthur's ineptitude should keep him out of the country for the next several months. If that doesn't prove to your dad that Arthur's a bumbling fool, nothing will."

Perry didn't say anything, merely sat down on one of the captain's chairs in the kitchen. Mitzie was happily coloring on the floor in the dining room. As was her custom, Mitzie had one eye on the picture she was coloring and one eye on Perry.

"Perry, didn't you hear me? I said your dad shipped Arthur out of the country. We know that his takeovers are one-man operations. We know there's nobody helping him. That means since your father sent him too far away to be trouble for anybody, Mike McGuire is safe for the time being.''

"That's wonderful," Perry said, then licked her lips.

"That also means you can come home."

For a few seconds, Perry didn't say anything, then she cleared her throat. "Well, I could, but then I'd lose my advantage."

"Your advantage!" Cora gasped. "Perry, you've already admitted that you're standing on thin ice with Mike McGuire. For Pete's sake, sooner or later, that man's going to realize you're buying his dinners at a restaurant! That advantage you're so proud of is nothing but pure luck."

"Not really," Perry said blithely. "Every day I learn something new. Pretty soon, I really will know what I'm doing."

Cora groaned. "Oh, no. You're starting to like it."

"I wouldn't say I like it," Perry said thoughtfully. "But it's interesting. Appealing in an odd kind of way."

"Perry, come home."

"No, I can't. I'm not ready to. Besides, I do think I should be here—firmly planted—when Arthur gets back. Look at it this way, Cora, by the time Arthur returns to Ebensburg, Mike McGuire will probably trust me."

"Or by the time Arthur gets back, Mike McGuire may have also discovered who you are."

"Oh, baloney. How could he possibly find out who I am?"

"The same way we found him. With a private investigator."

Perry sighed. There was a part of her that knew Cora had some valid points, and another part of her that disagreed completely. Arthur wouldn't simply give up on Mike McGuire's territory just because of an unexpected delay in his plans, and now more than ever, Perry wanted to be sure she could help Mike foil those plans. Which meant Mike had to trust her. And last night, they'd planted some very good seeds toward a bumper crop of trust. She couldn't leave now.

But there was also more to it than that. Something much more personal, much more valuable. Last night, she felt as if she'd held the first honest conversation of her life. Last night, she felt as if she'd received her first honest kiss. She was experiencing and discovering things she never knew existed and she wasn't ready to throw it all away yet.

"Cora," she asked suddenly, "do you realize what this little charade really is?"

"Yes, it's our way of showing your father Arthur's corrupt."

"On the surface, yes. But if you really examine the situation one step further, it's also my way of proving myself to my father."

"I don't understand."

"If I had already proven myself to my father, I wouldn't need to have evidence that Arthur's corrupt. All I'd need to do is voice my suspicions. Then Daddy would investigate."

"Perry, you've only been working with your father for six years and though you've come a long way in the business aspect, the dollars and cents and balance sheets, I hate to tell you this, but you still have a lot to learn about people."

"Exactly," Perry happily agreed. "And what that really boils down to is common sense."

Cora sighed. "Oh, Perry, I've known you too long not to see that you're about to tell me something I'm not going to like. So, please, just explain yourself before I have a heart attack jumping to all the wrong conclusions."

"Okay," Perry said seriously. "Mike and I had a little talk Friday night that somehow disintegrated into a discussion of my father. And that's when I realized Daddy didn't trust me."

"What in the devil were you and Mike McGuire doing talking about your father?" Cora gasped in disbelief.

"I was trying to get him to talk about himself, but we somehow ended up talking about Daddy. Cora, the conversation was so generic, Mike didn't catch any of it except that I was uncomfortable about my dad."

"Oh, Perry, please come home."

"You're not hearing what I'm telling you. Cora, I've spent the past six years at Omnipotence and my dad still doesn't trust me. But more than that, I'm now questioning myself. I've got to run that whole conglomerate someday and I'm not going to be able to do that if I don't get some common sense."

"And you've decided working as a housekeeper is the perfect way to get some common sense."

"Look how smart *you* are."

"Don't try to butter me up. This is serious. Your father will kill *me* if he finds out what I let you do."

"You just made my point," Perry said superiorly. "Even you admit my father won't punish me, but you, when he finds out about this plan, even though the plan was mine."

"Perry, that's because I've been your nanny since you were four and your father still—"

"Nobody thinks of me as me," Perry interrupted. "Just my father's daughter. Nobody thinks of me as a capable person. Just the person that they have to deal with because my father owns the company. But here, nobody knows who I am. Here, I am allowed to think for myself, make mistakes for myself and figure out the way to get out of those mistakes. I'm actually holding down a job. And not because my father owns the company."

"Perry, in case you're missing the obvious, you're only doing that job with my help."

"Yes, but you're not here for everything. There are plenty of things I've handled on my own."

"Really?" Cora asked sarcastically. "Like what?"

"I found the place that sells sandwiches in a bag," Perry said reasonably. "I shopped for my own clothes. I know to take the food out of the restaurant containers before I—"

"Perry, stop, please. I know what you're trying to tell me. Really, I do. Being Graham Pierson's daughter isn't easy. I think I understand that better than anybody. But what you don't seem to understand is that even though you're working very hard, even though you are gaining some valuable experience, the risks here are just too high. The minute *anybody* discovers you're *Pamela* Pierson, billion-dollar heiress, this situation turns into front-page news."

"I think the chance of that happening is very slim. And to me, the potential for gain far, far outweighs the possibility that someone will discover who I am."

Cora leaned back in her chair and sighed. "Perry, you know your father hates publicity of any kind. You also know how your father has reacted to the antics of other celebrities' offspring. I love you like one of my own children but Graham Pierson expects me to keep you on the straight and narrow. And until this morning, it seemed you also understood and respected that. So, what is it that you're not telling me?"

Perry cleared her throat. "Not telling you?"

"Come on, Perry, something serious has to have happened for you to be willing to put everybody out on a limb like this. Especially for you to be willing to risk embarrassing your father if anybody finds out."

"Who says I'm going to embarrass my father? No one is ever going to find out who I am."

Cora sat forward, resting her forehead on her palm. Knowing she'd never talk Perry out of this, she realized she had only one alternative. Perry wanted to be on her own, and Cora decided maybe it was time to give her exactly what she wanted. "Let's hope no one finds out who you are. Be-

cause the tabloids would just love to run a story about how
Graham Pierson's daughter worked as a housekeeper.
Goodbye, Perry. And good luck.''

With that, she hung up and, confused, Perry stared at the
silent phone. She hadn't expected Cora to be thrilled, but
she also hadn't expected the woman to desert her. Yet, that's
exactly what had happened. Cora had just deserted her. The
only person Perry truly counted as a friend had—albeit by
default—taken her father's side.

"Well, so be it," Perry mumbled and hung up the phone.
She could do this. She had to do this. Not only did she want
to learn, but for once, just once, she wanted to see how it felt
to be Perry. Not Graham Pierson's daughter.

After putting Mitzie to bed for her nap, Perry marched
into the laundry room. The wash hadn't been done for a
week and she wouldn't even have realized it if the twins
hadn't run out of clean underwear. She'd hoped to get help
from Cora, but since she didn't get the chance to ask for
any, she'd just figure this out for herself. That was, after all,
her new reason for being here. To learn. Even if that meant
making mistakes.

Sighing again, she grabbed the box of soap powder. The
directions read that she should add a cup and a quarter of
the powder for every load she washed. Glancing down
Perry realized she had at least seven loads of clothes, maybe
ten. She looked at the box again, then clicked her tongue.
Even the simplest things were so darned complicated.

Without bending, Perry began kicking the clothes into
small stacks. By looking into the washer's drum, she had a
fairly good idea of how many clothes would fit into a load
and she separated the one huge stack into ten small ones
without consideration for fabric or color, only size.

When the clothes were separated to the best of her ability, Perry examined the knobs of the washer trying to figure out what all the dials and numbers meant, and though

she never really figured out the intricacies of hot, warm, delicate and spin, a twist and a pull easily got the thing running. Water poured into the fat bowl and Perry again grabbed the detergent. Ten loads of clothes to wash meant she had to add ten cups of soap. At least that was simple enough.

She began to measure, pouring cup after cup into the water until she had the ten she needed, then she decided to add an eleventh cup just in case she'd miscounted. Then she remembered that each load took a cup and a quarter, not just a cup and she added another two and a half cups.

As water continued to stream into the washer, Perry bent, grasped the first load of clothes and stuffed them into the drum. She read the instructions on the washer one more time, glanced at the clothes, and, satisfied that she'd done her best, closed the lid and walked into the kitchen.

Luckily, Mitzie was asleep or the little girl would be jumping into the already separated stacks of clothes and Perry would have to separate them again. Now Perry actually got ten minutes of quiet time. She made another pot of coffee, sank into a captain's chair and, sipping warm, bitter coffee, decided it was time to create a plan.

If Cora was afraid of risking Graham Pierson's wrath, then Perry would simply keep her out of the picture. There'd be no more calls for help, no more calls for sympathy. Somehow, Perry would have to find a way to do everything herself.

And she'd handle this Arthur problem herself, too. Because not only did she want to protect Cora, but deep-down inside, she needed to prove herself to her father once and for all. Maybe if she could uncover the information alone, while she gathered a little common sense and people skills along the way, maybe then her father would finally trust her.

The washer began to twist and gyrate. In fact, it made such a god-awful sound, Perry went into the laundry room and opened the lid. The only possible explanation was that there were too many clothes in the drum, so she removed two pairs of Mike's jeans and after wringing excess water from them, tossed them into a laundry basket. She closed the lid and walked out of the laundry room just as Mike came flying into his kitchen via the back door.

"Of all the stupid..." He stopped short when he saw Perry standing in the laundry-room doorway.

Their eyes met for a painfully awkward moment. They hadn't been alone together since that kiss Friday night because Mike had spent most of the weekend doing yard work with the boys, and he'd left for the office this morning without even yelling goodbye into the kitchen. It hurt her that he could kiss her that way, then not face her for days afterward, but this was a real problem encountered by real women and, to be frank, Perry wasn't all that upset about having to deal with it. It was much better than wondering if the man in your life was only pursuing you because of your father's money.

Obviously uncomfortable, Mike looked away and Perry immediately noticed that his shirt was drenched with ink. "Oh, my gosh! What happened?"

"Stupid Sam," Mike growled. "He was holding his pen. Like this," he said, demonstrating that Sam had his pen by the end, the way one would hold a drumstick, very tightly so that it couldn't slide away. "And I was telling him... telling him... a story," he said, glancing away as he yanked off his suit jacket and tossed it to a waiting captain's chair. Walking to the sink, he began unbuttoning his shirt.

"And," Perry prompted when he stopped talking.

"And nothing," Mike decided. "It's not important." He removed his shirt, shoved it into the trash container under the sink and turned on the faucet to wash his hands.

"No! No!" Perry said, scampering to the sink. "This is important. Tell me about work. Really. I mean it. I've been here for a whole week, yet you've hardly told me anything about your job."

At that, Mike began to laugh. "Perry, you are so naive." He faced her then, his hairy chest just about eye level and definitely hand level, and Perry's blood turned to slow moving lava, even as her knees started to buckle. She licked her lips and took a pace back, but she couldn't pull her eyes away from his magnificently hairy chest.

"Can't you guess what I was telling Sam that made him snap his pen in two and splash ink all over my damned shirt without his even being slightly repentant?"

Managing to pull her gaze upward, Perry shook her head. "No."

"I was telling him about that kiss Friday night!" With very word he said, Mike took a step toward her and Perry began walking backward, away from him. He was angry—furious—because he found her attractive. And even though Perry could have taken that as an insult of sorts, that part of it didn't bother her as much as his misdirected anger.

It actually frightened her. Not because she was afraid of him. Instinctively, she knew he'd never hurt her. What frightened her was that his anger didn't inspire reciprocal anger, but rather some sort of sexual challenge to prove him wrong. To prove that this attraction wasn't bad, but good. And neither one of them was ready to deal with that right now.

Mercifully, the washer groaned and Perry gasped, spinning away from him. She ran to the laundry room but stopped short in the doorway. "Oh, my gosh!" she yelped, bounding into the room in the hope of stopping the washer, which was spitting mountains of soap out of the sides of its closed lid.

Of course, her tennis shoes didn't have enough traction for the slippery suds, and on first contact, her foot went sliding and Perry flew three feet in the air before she crash landed on a stack of teddy-bear pajamas and Ninja Turtle sheets.

Mike had followed her to the doorway and as he saw her mishap, he broke into gales of laughter. It had been such a miserable day. Such a horrible, rotten, miserable day that his funny bone was desperate for stimulation. And though he knew he shouldn't be laughing, he couldn't stop the chuckles from vibrating from him any more than the washer could stop spitting suds.

He laughed until his chest hurt, and the gentleman in him recognized that he was being more than a little bit rude. With a long breath to quell his laughter, he walked into the room and stood over Perry.

"Come on," he said, stifling another chuckle because she looked absolutely pitiful. Thick white suds framed her red hair and grew around her at a swift enough pace that Mike realized she'd be buried in about a minute and a half. "Let me help you up."

"No, thank you," she replied, righteously indignant. "I'll manage on my own."

"Come on," he jeered, bending forward enough that he could shove his outstretched hand at her. "Look, I'm sorry I laughed."

She slapped his hand away. "I didn't laugh at your shirt, I sympathized."

"I said I was sorry," Mike repeated and grabbed her wrist before she could pull it away from him. "Now, come on."

As he tugged on her hand to help her up, she tried to wrestle her arm from his grasp and the combination of forces, coupled with the wet, slippery suds, sent him flying to the floor. He landed with a hard thud on top of Perry and even though most of her breath had been knocked from her, she immediately pushed at him.

"Get off me!" she yelped. "I mean it. This is the last straw."

"I'm trying," he yelled right back at her. "Stop your damned wiggling and maybe I'll get my footing!"

"Get your damned footing and maybe I'll stop my wiggling."

Even to Perry that sentence sounded incredibly foolish and she stopped, glanced at Mike, who was studying her, cautiously trying to gauge her mood, and both of them burst into giggles. They laughed until their sides hurt, but as abruptly as their laughter started, it died. And when it died, they were staring at each other, not like two people lying in a puddle of warm, wet suds, but like two people who shared an undeniable hunger. Two people who couldn't stop it or put it off anymore.

As Mike bent to kiss her, Perry stretched to meet him. The touch of their lips sent wildfire to her heart and Perry slid her hands up his naked arms, along his smooth bare shoulders and into his shiny black hair so she could press his head down more firmly to her eager mouth.

But he wasn't happy with having her guide him and as she tried to bring him closer, he lightened the pressure of his mouth, yet his kiss became hungrier, greedier. The quick feathery brushes of his lips against hers ignited a passion within her of diametrically opposed proportions. The lighter his kiss, the stronger her desire, until she was meeting him, passionately, greedily and her hungry fingers weren't satisfied to touch only his hair.

She pulled her hands away, skimming his neck and shoulders as she branded a path to the wonderful chest she knew awaited her. The slow, yet determined course of her fingers inspired a new, more determined passion in his kiss, which became slow, decisive. Every movement of his mouth spoke to her in a language she'd never heard before, but when her fingers reached the thick black hair of his chest, he stopped, pulled away and looked down at her.

With their gazes locked, Perry dragged her fingernails from his neck to his navel, scraping through the thick forest of hair, raising gooseflesh not just on him, but on herself, as well. He watched her eyes as she made her initial exploration, then with her fingers resting just above his navel, he placed his fingers on top of her sweater, at the collar, and imitated her movement, gliding his fingers down her chest, between her eager breasts, along her stomach and to the place he must have imagined her navel would be.

When he stopped, they both simply looked at each other.

He was telling her that she was the master of this game. He'd go as far as she wanted to go.

No farther.

No faster.

Chapter Nine

With their eyes locked and their breathing slow, steady and very sure, Perry glided her hands up Mike's sides, feeling not just the supple skin beneath her hands but the warmth of him, an essence that somehow encompassed both the physical and emotional.

As if by mutual consent, their lips met again, in soft communication that was filled with love and tenderness. The tempo had changed, the pace had definitely slowed, because they were no longer two people incapable of harnessing their passion, they were now two people expressing a deep feeling. They were, in a very real sense, making a commitment to each other.

"Well, now, isn't this cozy."

Every muscle in Perry's body became stiff, and though her immediate reaction to the soft female voice was to jump up and perhaps run, Mike froze. She expected him to leap to his feet. He didn't. She expected him to look up. He didn't. He lay frozen, half-suspended above her. She felt his chest barrel out with a slow, deliberate intake of air, his beautiful blue eyes boring into her like two blue-white laser beams.

"Michael, I'll be at home waiting for you, when you're ready to talk about this."

Perry glanced at the doorway just in time to see the petite blonde wave her hand in disgust and turn toward the front hall. Still, Mike neither looked in the woman's direction, nor moved. He simply continued to stare at Perry. Both heard the front door open and close. Both heard the sounds of a car engine as it came to life. Both lay in the stillness that followed, neither moving, nor making a sound.

Finally, Perry cleared her throat and said, "Your mother?"

Continuing to do the unexpected, Mike braced his arms, then pushed himself away from Perry. "As if you didn't know."

Perry's face puckered in confusion and, twisting herself comically in the growing mound of soap suds, Perry also sat up. "How in the heck would I know your mother?"

"Will you stop it already!" Mike thundered as he whacked the knob on the washer and silenced it. "I know what's going on here. My mother hired you, remember?"

At that, Perry started to laugh. She laughed so hard, she slapped her thigh and soap suds flew around her. "I fired the woman your mother hired."

Mike pivoted to face her. "What?"

"I fired her," she repeated, still laughing. "Not only did Mitzie think she looked like the witch in 'Snow White,' but the woman announced that she wanted Mitzie put into daycare. She was dressed as if she were going to a museum, not about to clean house, and it was obvious she had absolutely no interest in taking care of Mitzie or making the place habitable. And though I know I didn't have the right to do it, I more or less showed her the door."

Stunned, Mike stared at her. "You're kidding?"

"No," Perry said, getting a little irritated with him now. "Don't you listen to anything I say?" She slapped her thigh again, this time trying to remove soap suds. "I told you. I am from out of town. *You* assumed I was your baby-sitter. *You* left me alone with Mitzie without allowing me to explain that I wasn't."

"Oh, my gosh," Mike said, leaning against the wall with a groan. "You're kidding."

"No, I am not kidding," Perry said, drawing in a deep breath as she glared at him. "About thirty seconds after you left, Mitzie came tripping down the steps and we made friends really quickly." She paused, considered her next statement and decided to say it, anyway. "Actually, I felt a bit sorry for her. She's such a sweet little thing and she was so excited to have a woman in the house again that when the wicked witch showed up, I simply couldn't leave Mitzie alone to suffer that fate. I honestly felt she deserved better."

There was a minute of silence, maybe two, and Perry rose and began separating the sopping wet clothes again. "You see, somehow it came out in conversation that my mother had died and Mitzie's mother had left and, well, I guess I overempathized with her."

"And stayed because you felt sorry for us."

Perry shook her head. "Not really. I didn't feel sorry for Mitzie until that horrid woman showed up. Then, after every plan I made sort of bombed, I realized I had the job, I wanted it, and I did."

Thoroughly confused, but genuinely interested, Mike said, "Why?"

"Because...because..." Perry threw her hands up in despair. "Oh, I don't know." She paused, sighed, then said, "I guess if I honestly analyze this right down to the bare

truth, I'd have to say my real life just isn't what it's cracke
up to be.''

"Are you saying that taking care of three kids, an old d
nosaur of a house and a grumpy newspaper editor some
how gives your life meaning?" he asked skeptically, peerin
at her as if she were crazy.

She smiled. "Actually, yes."

He shook his head in disbelief, then looked over an
smiled at her. "I hate to say this, but I'm feeling incredibl
complimented."

"You should be. You're very lucky, you know. No
everybody has great kids like yours. Good friends. Loy.
employees. Your life is very good."

Mike blew his breath out in a disgusted noise. "Hardl
That woman who just demanded my presence at her hom
to discuss this," he said, making the same sweeping motio
his mother had, though he hadn't seen it, but obviously w
familiar with the gesture. "That woman was my mothe
She can be a very domineering, very devious woman, wh
also has a very soft side, which makes me want to kill h
and hug her simultaneously."

"Sounds like my dad."

Mike slid down the wall, seating himself on the floor, u
ing the wall as a backrest. "I mean, just when I thir
everything's going to be okay, that she realizes I'm a grow
up and that she's going to be a good mother without bei
an overbearing mother, in she pops uninvited, unar
nounced and complaining."

Perry took a seat on the stack of damp clothes directly
front of him. "You wouldn't by any chance be an on
child?"

Rolling his eyes heavenward, Mike nodded.

"So am I."

"You said your mother's dead?"

"Yeah. She died when I was four. My dad hired Cora, who was my nanny and our housekeeper." Avoiding his eyes, Perry reached for one of Timmy's T-shirts and toyed with the sleeve. "Without Cora, I probably would have died of loneliness. I guess that's why I feel so much for Mitzie."

Reaching over, Mike put one finger under Perry's chin and lifted it, forcing her to face him. "Why is it you think that's bad?"

"I don't think it's bad," Perry said quietly, looking directly into his eyes. "I just think it sounds bad, or maybe it comes across improperly. I fell in love with Mitzie the minute I laid eyes on her. I didn't have to know she needed me, or that she was sad, I just instantly loved her. And though I don't understand it, I know in here," she said, pointing at her heart, "that I did."

Taking a deep breath, Mike rose and paced to the dry end of the laundry room. He made two trips across the only clean strip in the room, then turned and faced Perry again. When he spoke, it was softly. "My ex-wife was a very selfish, somewhat bitter woman, and I hate to say this, but when she left, I breathed a sigh of relief. I almost didn't care that I had to raise the kids alone, because I thought her negative influence was worse than no influence at all. But they missed something, not having a woman around. I recognize that every day when I come home and see how good you are with them. I very much appreciate your feelings for Mitzie and though you've been with us only a little over a week, I sense you have very strong feelings for the boys, as well."

"I do," she admitted with a nod.

"But," he continued, still softly, still with a great deal of hesitation. "You know . . . this thing between us is . . . very confusing."

Perry nodded slowly. "Yes, it is."

"And not really appropriate, considering that we live together."

Perry nodded again.

"I don't want you to get the wrong impression, here, but you're much more valuable to me as someone to love and care for my children than you are for... for... Well, than you are in any other capacity. So what do you say we sort of draw up some kind of truce."

"A truce?"

"Well," he said, then swallowed as if what he had to say was difficult. "Not really a truce, just a pact to keep things impersonal between us."

Perry started to laugh. "We have to make a pact to keep things impersonal? We can't go on the honor system?"

"Apparently not," Mike said, then he sighed. "We seem to have some sort of weird chemistry that I'm having a hell of a time controlling."

She gave him a puzzled frown, and he sighed again. "Look, even if we were dating, we shouldn't be kissing like that yet."

Perry smiled. "Been a long time since you dated, hasn't it?"

Mike started to laugh. "Actually, I think you've hit the nail on the head." He took a long breath, closed his eyes and then opened them again. "I have many, many problems in my life right now. And being attracted to you is a complication that I just can't handle."

She understood that perfectly, she didn't like it, but she understood. In fact, that even accounted for why he never questioned her about who she was. He was so wrapped up in his problems he not only missed the obvious, but part of him probably didn't want to deal with anything more than he had to right now. "Well," she said, then cleared her throat. "Then, let's just admit we find each other attractive and forget it. The whole thing's out in the open now, so there's no pretense. But that doesn't mean we have to be foolish, either."

He smiled with relief. "Yes, I agree a hundred percent."

When her very relieved employer offered her his hand to shake on the commitment, Perry didn't know whether to laugh or cry. Her first chance, maybe even her only chance, of seeing if a man could or would be interested in her, for her, not for her money, or her social position, or the power she had, was being tossed away because of circumstance.

And the worst part about it was, she had to agree with him.

Chapter Ten

After Mike left, Perry sat at the kitchen table, forlorn and despondent. She'd poured herself another cup of coffee, but it sat untouched, as Perry stared at nothing, unable to reconcile herself to the truce they'd made. Though it was true Mike would probably now consider his work a safe topic of conversation, and it was also true the chemistry was more than a little bit difficult to deal with, the deep relationship she suspected they could share wouldn't reach half the potential they had. The very best she could hope to accomplish when this whole charade panned out was that she'd have a very good friend. The thought didn't comfort her nearly as much as she hoped it would and she sprang from the table, bounded through the dining room, through the den and into the living room, where she began to pace.

Yawning and rubbing her eyes, Mitzie appeared in the doorway. "What are you doing?" she asked sleepily.

"Uh, I'm going to clean," Perry answered with the most logical thought that came to mind.

"The rug?" Mitzie asked, walking into the room.

Glancing down at the worn gold carpeting, Perry decided that probably wouldn't be such a bad idea because she'd actually cleaned very little since her first day. She'd dusted and vacuumed every room, including this one, but a real housekeeper would consider that only superficial touch-ups and with Arthur out of the country and her presence here more than a short-term visit, Perry realized she'd better start earning her keep or she wouldn't earn Mike McGuire's trust.

Humming a tune he made up as he went, Mike entered the door of the offices for the paper. The bell tingled but otherwise the world was silent, and when he glanced around at the familiar faces, all of which were staring at him with what seemed to be a sense of frightened anticipation, Mike froze.

"Don't tell me I missed the story of the century."

Sam cleared his throat. "No. But any one of us would be more than happy to take a steno pad into your office just in case you strangle your mother, who's waiting for you, reading everything on your desk, as we speak."

Anger welled up inside Mike, but he harnessed it. "I don't think that'll be necessary," he said, but he laughed. In a sense, the situation was becoming funny and perhaps he could put an end to this interfering, once and for all. Particularly, after he told his mother that her meddling days could cease. He'd found the housekeeper of his dreams. A housekeeper who loved Mitzie.

Straightening his shoulders, Mike marched into his office. His mother looked up from reading Mike's latest editorial, which was still in the typewritten stages, then rose and walked around his desk to meet him in the doorway and greet him with a kiss on the cheek.

"Well, Mother, what a pleasant surprise."

Smiling, Mary McGuire walked back to Mike's desk but this time she took a seat on the visitor's side rather than sit in his chair as she had been when he entered the room. "Darling, right after I left your house this afternoon, I called Robbin Farrington and discovered that she's not working for you. I know you probably think my unannounced appearance was incredibly rude, but the truth is I simply wasn't apprised of the whole situation. Now that I am, we can discuss this housekeeper misunderstanding openly and get it all straightened out."

Forcing a smile, Mike walked behind his desk and sat on his chair. "I'm afraid there was no misunderstanding, Mother."

"Oh, but there was," Mary insisted. "You see, Robbin was a little late for her first day of work and your *friend* apparently thought that was reason enough to dismiss her."

"My *friend* told me that Ms. Farrington frightened Mitzie." Though Perry hadn't said those words, being Mitzie's father, Mike was well aware that when Mitzie compared someone to the witch in "Snow White," she was afraid of them.

"Nonsense. Robbin didn't frighten Mitzie."

"Well, whether she did or didn't doesn't really matter anymore. I already have a housekeeper," he said, but didn't add anything about the obvious because though he and Perry had come to an agreement, that was something his mother would never understand. And unless or until she mentioned what she'd walked in on in the laundry room, Mike would run on the assumption that she was wise enough to realize it was none of her business.

"Yes, well," his mother said, leaning forward on her seat so that she could rest her arms on his desk. Her pale yellow hair shone in the sunlight pouring in his office window and her blue eyes sparkled. She was so pretty and so delicate that it was sometimes hard to believe she could be so devious.

"That's what I came to talk to you about. You see, Robbin didn't really get a fair chance."

Rubbing his fingers under his nose, Mike sat back in his chair and closed his eyes. "Mother," he said quietly, "can I ask you a question?"

"Of course, dear," his mother responded sweetly.

"This Robbin Farrington, is she by any chance incredibly attractive?"

"Oh, my goodness, yes! Why not only was she the second runner-up in the Miss Pennsylvania beauty pageant, but she seriously considered a modeling career."

"And is this the kind of woman you want raising your grandkids?"

"I beg your pardon?"

Sitting up, Mike opened his eyes and leaned across his desk until he and his mother were only inches apart. "Think about what you're doing here, Mom." Mike only called her "Mom" on certain occasions. She usually preferred to have him call her "Mother," but every once in a while, his calling her "Mom" seemed to soften her or please her. "You hired a socialite to work as a housekeeper in a farmhouse and to be the nanny for ten-year-old twins and a four-year-old who still thinks mud is an acceptable toy."

Mary stiffened. "Robbin was a nanny in Alexandria. And eventually, she would have made a fine housekeeper."

"No, in your thinking, she would have made a fine wife."

That obviously set Mary's mind working, and after a few seconds she deflated.

Mike smiled. "You're beginning to agree with me."

Dropping her hands to her lap, Mary gave in. "Darn."

It was at times like this that Mike understood how he could love his mother, despite the fact that she was a genius at minding other people's business and therefore making their lives miserable. Her motives were good, genuine, basically pure, but she didn't always think every situation through to its logical conclusion, and that's why she caused so much trouble.

Rising, Mike sighed sympathetically, then walked around his desk. Leaning his hip against its top, he faced his mother again. "Mother, I understand that you were only trying to help."

"You did ask me to use my influence to assist you in finding a housekeeper."

"And I appreciated the time and effort you put into that. In fact, I very much blame myself for this little disagreement because I should have handled it myself."

"I just want you to be happy."

"I know that."

"I don't like the kids being alone."

"They're not alone. In fact, we're actually a very happy family."

She looked at him pointedly. "And I don't like *you* being alone."

"I'm not alone. I have three kids and an entire newspaper staff to keep me company."

"And the woman I saw you with this afternoon," his mother reminded him, looking up at him expectantly.

"And this is where the conversation ends," Mike decided, pushing himself away from the desk.

With a quick motion of her slim hand, Mary stopped him. "Not so fast. I'm assuming this woman *is* the new housekeeper."

He didn't have to answer to her, Mike knew that, but he also knew that if he didn't answer at least some basic questions, she'd hound him to death.

"Yes. My new housekeeper's name is Perry Pierson," he said, giving his mother the surname Mitzie had relayed after Perry's second day of employment.

"And you like her," Mary prompted, motioning with her hand.

Inclining his head, Mike agreed. "Yes, I like her."

"As more than a housekeeper," she said, pushing him a little further.

"Well, let's put it this way. I *could* like her as more than a housekeeper."

"But?"

"But," he repeated, then walked away from her. "But I have too much on my mind right now to get involved with anyone—especially with someone who's living with me."

"She's living with you!" Mary gasped.

"Mother, it's very convenient to have a live-in housekeeper, and I shouldn't have to explain that to you. She reads to Mitzie, she does homework with the boys. To my way of thinking, I'm probably the luckiest man in the county to have found someone willing to work almost twenty-four hours a day."

"Don't talk to me about convenient, Michael McGuire...."

"That's it, Mother. That's as far as this conversation goes, because what I do with my life is my business, and I don't want you interfering."

Mary gasped again. "Don't you use that tone with me! I'm your mother! It's my responsibility—"

"No, it's not. Not anymore. I'm a grown person and Perry is a good housekeeper, and I want you to stay out of this."

From the expression on her face, Mike could tell his mother hadn't just heard every word he'd said, she also understood he meant business. For thirty seconds, she said absolutely nothing, then she shook her head and sighed. "You really want me to stay out of this."

"Precisely."

"Completely?"

Mike didn't waste a second. "Completely."

Sighing, Mary rolled her eyes heavenward. "Can I at least ask a few questions?"

He took a deep breath. "What kind of questions?"

"Well, for one, where is she from? Do you know her family? Do *I* know her family? How old is she? Has she gone to college?"

"Mother, that wasn't a few questions. That was at least four."

"Which actually proves a point," Mary said, shaking a red-tipped finger at her son. "There are many more things to consider here than how pretty she is."

Finding the flaw in his mother's thinking, Mike smiled. "You're right, because Perry's looks have nothing to do with how well she does her job. And, in fact, the reason I keep her is because of her tenacity."

Mike's mother frowned. "Her tenacity?"

"Sure. She's not a housekeeper. She worked in a hospital in Boston—"

"She's a nurse?" Mary interrupted.

"No, she was in administration. Anyway, I'm not sure how she ended up at my house, maybe she saw my ad when she was passing through, but when she came to the house, I thought she was the baby-sitter and left her with Mitzie, and..."

"Why in the devil would an obviously educated woman take a job as a housekeeper?"

"To be honest, I think she was bored. Or maybe disillusioned with her life. Anyway..."

"Oh, boy!"

"Mother, stay out of it. I know it sounds odd, farfetched and even ridiculous." He couldn't believe he was saying these things out loud. Worse, he couldn't believe he agreed with them. "But the whole point is, Perry loves Mitzie and Mitzie loves Perry, the boys actually asked me to choose books for them to read to help them fall asleep and I don't have to worry about my household for the first time in three years."

"Michael, you've lost your perspective."

"Oh, yeah. I get this from the woman who thinks hiring the second runner-up in the Miss Pennsylvania contest is the way to find a housekeeper."

"Okay. Okay, so I'm a snoopy old woman, but I'm also your mother, and since I've lived fifty-six years, I'm also a little wiser than you. And I'm telling you something's wrong here."

"Nothing is wrong here."

"At least find out a little bit about her family."

"I don't need to know a little bit about her family. She's my housekeeper!"

"Frankly, Michael, I think the fact that she's rooming with you is very much cause for investigation."

"Why? Do you think she's going to steal the silver?"

"You don't know that she won't," Mary said reasonably. "Because you know nothing about her past."

"All right, I know that she's from Boston. I know that her mother died when she was four. And I know she worked in a hospital."

"And her family?"

"Why are you so concerned about her family?"

"Because you never know. What if her father is a gangster? What if her brother steals? What would you do if you came home one day and found Mitzie bouncing on the knee of a drunkard?"

"It's very unfair to judge someone by their relatives."

"And it's very convenient that her family's not around. Do you think she could, perhaps, be ashamed of them? Are you sure she wasn't actually a janitor at that hospital? Good people from good families don't just up and run away. And, Michael, that's what she's done. She's run away."

"No, she hasn't. It's not like that at all."

"Then prove it to yourself. Prove it to all of us. Clear her name. Hire an investigator."

Mike's mouth fell open in surprise. "What?"

"You heard me. Hire an investigator. Find out who she really is."

"I can't believe you said that."

"You're just afraid of the truth."

"And you're just dying to know what's wrong with her because I like her and the kids like her."

That comment made her smile. "See, even you admit there's something wrong."

Chapter Eleven

Despite the fact that Mike was well accustomed to his mother's meddling, he had to admit that her visit had disturbed him to a degree and that she had made some valid observations. It was very odd to allow an uninvestigated stranger to live in your home. In fact, the suspicions his mother had planted in his mind bothered him so much that Mike decided to go home early. He wasn't really sure what he was going to say or even what he was hoping to find. All he knew was, like it or not, his mother had a point.

"Good afternoon," he said, walking into the kitchen through the opening provided by the swinging door. But he stopped abruptly when he saw the picture before him. This baby-sitter, this housekeeper/baby-sitter who'd just landed in his home out of the blue, was actually reading the directions on a bag of frozen french fries.

"What are you doing?"

Perry glanced up at him. "I'm reading directions," she said casually, as though it were the most normal thing in the world.

"For frozen french fries?" he asked incredulously.

"Sure," she replied, smiling at him. He would have been devastated by that smile, but he refused, ordered himself to remember his priorities, and he won because he realized he'd been so caught up in this woman's attractiveness, that he was missing, ignoring or downplaying the fact that she wasn't much of a housekeeper. She might be a great baby-sitter, but the truth of the matter was, she'd hardly done more than a superficial housecleaning, and he really couldn't say she'd actually cooked. When he evaluated their menu one meal at a time, in the week she'd been here, they'd eaten frozen food dinners and cold cuts. This was the item drifting in his subconscious that never quite surfaced, and probably why his mother's warning haunted him.

"You know, all frozen french fries are not created equal," she continued in a serious, almost chastising voice, as if he were the one with the problem, not her. "We can micro-wave these, we can cook them in the oven or we can fry them in oil, depending upon the way we want them to taste."

He stared at her. He'd never seen anyone read the direc-tions for cooking frozen french fries, let alone take them so much to heart. And despite the obvious, he couldn't be-lieve she was doing it now. "What are you talking about?"

"If you're watching your cholesterol, and everybody should be, we really don't want to set these in oil—which we would have to do to fry them."

"Okay," he said, dragging the little word out into sev-eral long syllables and watching her as she took a pair of scissors and made a clean swipe across the top of the plastic bag.

"But if we just set them on a cookie sheet and place them in the oven for—" she glanced at the bag "—twenty-five minutes, we'll have nice crispy fries, with no added choles-terol."

As she spoke, she glanced over at him and smiled slightly, the same way an actor on a commercial would look into the camera when he or she delivered the big finish. Mike shook his head. This couldn't be for real. The only explanation was that his mother now had him so suspicious, he was throwing everything out of proportion in the other direction. Maybe he should change his clothes, seek out Mitzie and watch the late-afternoon cartoons. Maybe after an hour or so of mind-numbing entertainment, he'd get his perspective again and be able to look at this situation objectively.

"Well, don't let me disturb you and your low-cholesterol fries," he said, backing toward the stairway. "Just give me a call when dinner is ready. I'm going to change, then Mitzie and I will be in the living room watching cartoons."

Perry had been so preoccupied with the french fries that she hardly heard what he'd said. When the full implication of his statement sunk in, Perry's heart stopped and as quickly as it stopped, it jumped into overtime. "Wait!" she yelled, scampering toward the stairwell. She couldn't let this man set one foot into his living room because the rug was soaking wet and reeked of pine cleaner. One look at the mess she'd made and all truces and agreements from the morning before would be off because they wouldn't need them. He'd fire her, and then not only would she lose her slim chance of getting his friendship, she'd also lose the chance to catch Arthur. "Stop!" she yelled again.

This time, her efforts were rewarded, and her employer turned to face her. His blue eyes were wide and it appeared as if his breathing had stopped. Obviously, the tone of her voice had scared the devil out of him. "What?"

"I . . . I'm sorry," Perry said quietly, contritely. "I didn't mean to scare you, but Mitzie's not upstairs."

"Maybe not, but my clothes are. And I want to change."

"That reminds me," Perry said brightly, inspiration striking as suddenly as the first raindrop from heaven. She'd

keep this man busy and out of the living room if it killed her
"Most of your clothes are still in the one closet of my—the
bedroom you're letting me use."

His face changed. Slowly, every one of his facial muscles
melted from their almost frozen state caused by his fright
and shifted into a cautious, but somehow stern expression
"And?"

In spite of the look he was leveling at her, Perry continued to smile. Her lips trembled, her heart pounded, but she
smiled, anyway. There was no way she'd let this man know
she feared getting fired. If she allowed him to see that, it
would make him realize she had reason to fear getting fired
and he'd soon see every one of her mistakes, not just the
obvious ones.

"And since Mitzie's outside playing, I thought perhaps
this might be a good time for you to remove the things you
use the most frequently, so we don't have to...have to...you
know."

"Worry about bumping into each other."

Clearing her throat, she nodded. "You could let Mitzie
stay outside while you move your clothes."

"No."

Her heart stopped. "No?"

With a deep breath, he jogged down the stairs, then
walked toward the back door. "No, I think I'll have Mitzie
help me make the exchange. Because of the yard work I've
been busy doing I haven't spent any more than ten minutes
alone with her in the last three days, and this is as good a
way as any to make up for that."

Not waiting for a reply, he pushed on the screen door and
exited the house.

Perry breathed a long sigh of relief and collapsed against
the refrigerator, but, just as quickly, she realized that she
hadn't solved the problem, only delayed the inevitable. She
had her doubts that the rug would be dry by the time Mike

finished moving his clothes, and though she could keep the family out of the living room for hours because of dinner, dishes and homework, she wasn't sure even that would be enough time to dry a carpet that had puddles in its nap.

Mike agreed with Perry that he would get his things out of her bedroom, but he wasn't going to venture into that room alone and he wasn't going to ask Perry to help him. There was no way in hell he wanted to be alone in a bedroom with that woman; it would send all his senses into overdrive again, and he had to have a clear head so he could evaluate her objectively.

All he needed was a little tour guide. Someone who could direct him away from drawers that contained personal, private, womanly things. And as he pushed open the door to the master bedroom, he assured himself the giggling little girl he was holding could fit the bill.

"Okay, Mitzie," he said as he bounced her to the floor. "Do you know if Perry's using any of these drawers?"

Blue eyes round and serious, Mitzie blinked up at him. "Uh-uh."

"What do you mean, uh-uh? Haven't you ever seen her pull a sweatshirt out of a drawer?"

"Uh-uh," Mitzie said, then spun away from him and leaped on the bed. "Can I jump?"

"No, you cannot jump," Mike said, disturbed because he recognized Mitzie knew better than to even ask.

"Not even a little bounce?"

"Not even a little bounce."

She sighed heavily, said, "Okay," then snuggled against the quilt Mike realized she associated with her mother. One of the few stories he could tell Mitzie about her mother was that while she was pregnant with Mitzie, she'd bought that quilt. Otherwise, Elaine had pretty much ignored her pregnancy and her third child.

"All right. Just a little bounce."

"Okay!" Mitzie yelped, scrambled to her feet and immediately started bouncing. She went far beyond the bounds of a little bounce, but Mike overlooked it. When it came to remembering that Mitzie's mother really and truly hadn't wanted her, Mike always ended up with a soft spot in his heart for the baby girl he knew looked just like him.

"All Perry's underwear's in that bag," Mitzie announced suddenly, bringing Mike's attention back to the project at hand. And, as if by magic, when his mind focused in on that project, he started smelling things. Powder. Cologne. Even her deodorant had a nice light floral scent. He didn't have to bring his nose up against anything. The scents just sort of happened. When he was by the dresser that held the cologne, one deep breath brought the scent to his nose. When he entered the bathroom and stepped by the sink, which held her deodorant, two short sniffs brought that aroma into the air. Approaching the bathtub, he saw the open box of powder sitting on the rim, and he stooped, bringing the enticing fragrance to his nostrils via three quick waves of his hand. Light, white granules billowed a fraction of an inch from the container and he watched them, as if mesmerized.

"I'm done bouncing."

The sound of Mitzie's voice spoken directly into his left ear shoved an arrow straight into Mike's heart. For a second, he thought he'd die from the paralyzing pain of being caught, but unconcerned, Mitzie turned away.

"Okay, kid," he said, feeling incredibly foolish and really paranoid. "Let's grab some of the things I need and be on our way."

"Okay," Mitzie agreed blithely. Without a second's hesitation, she walked to a drawer, pulled it open and scooped out an armload of socks. "I'll do the socks."

"Good," Mike said as he walked over to the taller dresser. He opened the first drawer and pulled out T-shirts, which he stacked on the bed. Realizing the slowness of this process, Mike grabbed two clothes baskets from the hall. He handed one to Mitzie and kept one for himself, and basket by basket he and Mitzie shifted the contents of his dresser drawers from one room to the other.

"Well, Mitzie," he announced, taking a deep breath, which puffed his chest out with pride. "I'd say we're done."

"Except for the closet."

"We can do that tomorrow."

"Okay," Mitzie agreed. "I'll go help Perry now."

Mike nodded, smiling. "Okay."

Mitzie scampered out of the room and Mike began to follow her, but as he reached the door, he realized that it would be much simpler to get his work clothes for tomorrow right now so that he wouldn't have to sit on the edge of his bed waiting for the sound of Perry tiptoeing down the stairs in the morning or ask permission to go into her bedroom later that night. He turned and made his way back to his closet, but his hand grasped the wrong doorknob, and as the door opened, he didn't see a row of shirts and trousers, but rather the green satin nightgown and exquisite paisley robe.

It was probably the most beautiful, most feminine outfit he had ever seen, and the funny part about it was, it was not blatantly sexy, it certainly wasn't revealing, and, in fact, looking at it as it hung before him, Mike could almost say it was literally a very innocent garment.

But that was actually what made it so beautiful. It was a very normal thing a very normal woman wears and Mike had long denied himself the privilege of being around a woman. He was an absolutely normal man, pretending, or trying to pretend women didn't exist, and now it was backfiring because he had a feminine, attractive woman under his roof, in his bed, using his bathtub.

But, at least now he knew why he found it difficult to deal
with Perry. It wasn't her. She might be beautiful—very
beautiful—but she, personally, wasn't the reason for the
breakdown of his ability to resist her. The problem was
proximity. He'd sheltered himself from women for too long,
and now he was being forced to deal with her existence. Deal
with the fact that men liked women. Craved women. Were
attracted to women. And he'd acted like an adolescent instead of handling this the way mature men handled their
normal attraction to women. They didn't avoid or ignore the
entire gender, they controlled themselves. They acted like
adults, not like teenagers who finally realized the differences between men and women were good, not bad.

Now, he would, too.

He took one last, longing look at the beautiful nightgown and robe and as he did, the strangest thing hit him.
The only other item in the closet was the dress she'd worn
Friday night. And Mitzie had said her underwear was in a
bag. Confused, he took another look in the closet, then
glanced around the room for suitcases. He didn't see any.

Boiling hot dogs was what Perry considered a gift from
God. Baking french fries ranked as a close second. Prepar-
ing vegetables from a can wasn't exactly a difficult task, either, but buying coleslaw from a deli was inspired. Not only
did the coleslaw provide a less generic look to the meal, it
actually tasted good, too. And everything she'd bought
could be prepared in under ten minutes. A blessing for a
woman who needed all her mental energy to come up with
a reason that Mike shouldn't have his TV time tonight.

"Okay, dinner's ready," Perry called up the stairs as the
boys bounded into the kitchen from the Coopers'. "Wash
your hands," she ordered sweetly, smiling at the twins.

They mumbled agreements, ran to the powder room and returned before the senior McGuire and his daughter had come downstairs.

Again, Perry called up the stairs, "Come on, you two, dinner will get cold if you don't hurry."

Mitzie scrambled down the steps. "Dad's still in your room."

Perry wasn't sure why, but the thought struck her as odd. Perhaps because Mitzie had returned without him. "Don't touch anything," she ordered. "I'll be back in two minutes."

She ran up the steps, but before she reached the top, Mike walked out of the room she'd been using. He held an armload of clothes that had been hanging in his closet, and when he saw her, he stopped walking and just stared at her.

"Dinner's ready," she said quietly.

He cleared his throat. "Okay."

"Is something wrong?" she ventured uncertainly.

He didn't answer for a minute, then took a long breath and said, "No. Everything's fine."

Everything wasn't fine. She could tell by the look on his face that something was terribly wrong. And the only thing she could figure out was that he realized she'd manipulated him into clearing his clothing out of her bedroom and that there must be a reason she'd done that. Maybe it would be best to simply tell him the truth, admit she'd soaked his rug with pine cleaner by trying to scrub it with the mop, the same way Cora had taught her to scrub the kitchen floor.

She cleared her throat. "Well, I know you probably guessed already that I sort of kept you from the cartoons for a reason."

"Really?" he asked, his eyebrows raising. "I hadn't noticed, but now that you mention it . . ."

Gathering her courage, Perry took a long breath, ready to make a full confession about the rug, but Mike beat her

to the punch. "Save it until after dinner," he said, turning
in the direction of his temporary bedroom and walking away
from her.

In that second, Perry didn't just understand, she actually
felt the meaning of the phrase "moment of truth." They'd
eat and get the children settled before they held this discussion because her employer realized that this situation was
serious enough that he'd probably end up firing her, and he
wouldn't do that in front of the kids.

Chapter Twelve

"I tried to scrub the rug."

They'd finished dinner several minutes ago, Mike had assigned the boys to dish duties and given Mitzie a coloring book and a box of crayons. Now, he and Perry stood in the doorway of the living room, staring at the wet, incredibly piney rug.

Digesting the information she'd just given him, Mike turned to her. "With pine cleaner?" he asked incredulously.

She sighed with misery. "It worked in the kitchen."

He could see that she was genuinely concerned that she may have ruined his carpet and that she was greatly upset by the prospect. Worse, given that this error would undoubtedly come down to the conversation both of them had been trying to avoid, which would upset her even more, Mike decided it might be best to handle the rug emergency before they actually sat down and discussed the real problem. "Okay. Don't panic. From now on, just remember you don't use pine cleaner on a rug. And, in fact, you don't use a mop.''

She nodded.

''I'm going to run out to the hardware store and rent a carpet cleaner, then you and I will take care of this. We can't let a sopping wet rug sit all night.''

She nodded again.

''So, you help the boys with their homework, get Mitzie bathed and read her a story. By that time, I should be back with the machine.''

She nodded yet again, and when Mike left, she slid down the wall in absolute agony. If this wasn't a dead giveaway that she was a member of a servant-filled aristocracy, nothing was. Now, she had absolutely no choice but to tell him the truth. The only question was, should she do it while they were sweating and scrubbing, or should she wait until they were done and both so tired, he wouldn't be able to scream at her. Or, better yet, should she wait until morning? She decided to tell him when they were finished.

At eleven that night, with all the living-room furniture sitting in the den and hallway, when both were so exhausted they couldn't move from their positions of being propped up against opposite walls in the dining room, Perry knew the time had come.

''I guess you figured out I never cleaned a rug before.''

''It wasn't really hard.''

''And I guess you realize I'm not a housekeeper.''

''You admitted that yourself.''

''Please, you've already done more than anybody should be expected to do for their housekeeper and I feel bad enough. Don't make this confession easy on me.''

He rose to his knees, crawled across the dining room and took up residence on the wall beside Perry. Casually, as if it were the most natural thing in the world, he slid his arm around her shoulders.

"Perry, I really don't care that you're not a housekeeper."

She glanced at him. "You don't?"

"No. I'm very impressed and pleased with the way you care for Mitzie and the twins, and basically, that would probably be enough to allow you to keep your job, if it weren't for the other inequities."

"Inequities?"

"It's just so damned convenient that you were here when I needed someone. You have no suitcases, and there are no clothes in the closet except the two things I've seen. I don't doubt for one minute that the woman my mother hired was inappropriate for the job, and I have no doubt that it was in my best interest that you fired her. But don't you think it's just a little too coincidental that you were here—ready and willing to become a housekeeper—in the exact second that you fired mine?"

Perry licked her lips. She knew he deserved an honest answer; she also knew neither one of them was ready for the complete truth yet. This was an explanation a wise woman eased her way into gradually. "What would you say if I told you that it was something like a happy accident that I came here that morning?"

Mike laughed. "In some respects, it's obvious I already believe that."

"Yes, but I don't think you understand how much of a happy accident it was from *my* vantage point."

"Why? Don't you think I'm smart enough to have figured out that finding a job with room and board would be like heaven to someone who's running away from a bad situation?"

Perry grimaced. "My situation really isn't that *bad*."

"Yes, but you are running, aren't you?"

Though she hadn't realized it until a few days before
Perry nonetheless knew that was somewhat true. She might
be trying to impress her father by cornering Arthur, but the
truth of the matter was, even if Arthur was out of the picture, she didn't think she could go home until she figured
out how to make her father trust her. "Yes, to be honest
with you, I am. My problems aren't serious or earth
shattering, but they are the reason I left Boston. I had only
intended to be gone for a day, but then you assumed I was
your baby-sitter and before I knew it, I was knee-deep in
Mitzie's problems. When I realized I couldn't get out of the
situation without making it look like Mitzie had done
something horrible to your baby-sitter, I also began to think
that maybe it wouldn't be such a bad idea for me to stay here
for a while. To take a little time to gather my wits before I
went back home."

Mike blew his breath out on a long sigh and fell back
against the wall. "Believe it or not, that's something of a
relief."

"It makes you happy to find out I need to gather my
wits?"

"No, it just makes more sense, that's all. For all I knew
you could have been fleeing from a bank robbery, a bad
marriage or even a murder, or something. But it sounds like
you're simply going through a normal life crisis. Would it
help to talk?"

She shrugged. "I don't know."

He didn't really feel that he was snooping or prying, even
though he knew this conversation would please his mother.
Every good employer knows it's wiser to help an employee
with a personal problem than to let it fester until it affects
their work. So, his curiosity was purely professional when
he encouraged her with an understanding smile. "Come on,
let's talk."

After a long breath, she rested her head against the wall behind them and said, "I don't know where to begin."

"Is it a love problem, a home problem, a parent problem, a job problem?"

She started to laugh. "Actually, it's all of them."

"No wonder you left."

"You don't understand. You couldn't understand because I look around me and what I see is perfection."

Mike laughed. "Huh! I look around and I see a hundred-year-old house badly in need of repair, a company that's teetering on the brink of disaster because of a pest who's trying everything in his power to bring it there, and kids who need more time, affection and attention than one person can give them."

"I think you do a wonderful job."

"You do?" he asked skeptically.

"Oh, God, yes. I already told you that my father was never home when I was a child, but what I didn't tell you about were the women who sometimes accompanied him when he did come home."

"Uh-oh. That doesn't sound too good."

"A new woman almost every month, and each and every one of them vying to be my stepmother. I got presents, I got sloppy kisses, I got unwanted trips to the zoo."

"Must have been hell," Mike said, then he laughed.

"It was," Perry insisted, glaring at him. "You try dealing with a bunch of gushing females, all wanting to become your new mom."

Mike had already realized that Mitzie and Perry had formed an immediate bond because they were very much alike, so it was Mitzie he pictured dealing with the gushing females, and when he did, he laughed with glee.

Perry slapped him with an available throw pillow, which had tumbled from the couch when they'd moved it to the den. "Stop that, it wasn't funny."

"No, I'm sure it wasn't," he agreed and then forced himself to adopt a more serious demeanor. "So, what about your other problems, the more recent problems?"

"Oh, they're stupid."

"No, they're not. They're not stupid if they caused you enough pain that you left."

"Yes, they are," Perry insisted, but she did so more out of a desire to avoid the conversation than to downplay her problems. She couldn't explain that her father didn't trust her, unless she told Mike about Arthur Tyrone, and though she had a very strong sense that talking about this with Mike would help her to put it into perspective, she couldn't jeopardize the housekeeping position she'd only two minutes ago saved.

Mike knew he had to push forward. She was avoiding something, something important, and until she really came clean with him, Mike knew he'd always have his doubts, and as long as he had doubts, neither one of them would have a moment's peace. "Well, at least tell me about your love problems."

Glancing at him, Perry began to giggle. "Actually, they're very similar to my would-be stepmother problems."

"Really?"

"Just replace the bunch of gushing females with a bunch of drooling men. Hundreds of potential suitors all tripping over themselves to have me on their arm at a charity function. It was pitiful."

He knew exactly what Perry was saying because if he hadn't gotten a hold of himself, he would have been one of those drooling men. In fact, he had been a drooling man—several times, if he were honest. "Perry, you're beautiful. I can understand why men tripped all over themselves to get to you."

She'd never looked at it that way. But when she did, she realized that was every bit as shallow a reason for wooing her as trying to get in good with her father, or trying to get part of her father's money. "That doesn't make it any easier to bear. Once, just once, I'd like for a man to get to know me, really get to know me, and like me—for me—before he asked me out."

That melancholy statement hit him, fast and hard, with an icy stab of guilt in the pit of his stomach. Though he'd never asked her out, he'd kissed her—passionately. And not just once, twice. Never mind that she'd kissed him back, never mind that she seemed to have been expecting it, he was every bit as culpable for the wistful note in her voice, as every man who'd caused her to leave her home.

"I'm sorry."

Perry glanced at him. "For what? None of this is your fault."

"Yes, I know, but basically I think I've been as insensitive as everyone else in your life."

"No, you haven't. You've been wonderful."

She gave the compliment quietly, honestly, and Mike got one of those pangs of attraction that coupled physical and emotional needs in such a way that the two almost felt like the same thing. In that exact second, he knew that if the conversation went any further, he'd try to kiss her again. And he couldn't do that. Not only did they have a truce in effect, but if he didn't adhere to that truce, he wasn't any better than the men she'd left behind. As close as he might feel to her right now, he really didn't know her well enough to love her, and unless he could really love this woman, he'd only add to her pain by making advances he couldn't yet back up with promises.

Besides, Mike knew Perry would be leaving. She had another life in another city, and though she might have chosen to leave that life, even she admitted that her absence was only temporary. He'd never be so foolish as to make the same mistake he'd made with Elaine. Until a woman could come to him unencumbered by a past and without regrets about a lost future, he didn't want her.

With a deep breath and a great deal of longing for things that couldn't be, Mike rose from his seat by the wall. "Well, there's nothing more we can do here. Let's just call it a night. We'll move the furniture back in the morning."

Chapter Thirteen

Three weeks later, when October winds had blown all the colored leaves from the trees and the temperatures dipped so far at night Perry had to buy flannel pajamas, Perry's secret was as safe as it had been on her first day of employment. Unfortunately, as much of a comfort as that was, it was also equally irritating.

She and Mike seemed to be friends, really good friends. They laughed with the kids, made dinner together, even watched TV, silently, companionably, as if they were... well, as if they were married, actually. But they never really talked. It drove her absolutely, positively crazy that they could be so close, yet, he didn't want to know who she was. Having someone treat her well without knowing anything about her, as if who she was was of no consequence, was almost as bad as having someone fall in love with her because of who she was.

Confused, and unwilling to remain that way, Perry grabbed her new blue ski jacket from the foyer closet,

strapped Mitzie behind a seat belt and drove to Janette
Cooper's house. Once Mitzie was happily settled behind the
wooden fence, playing with the beagles, Perry jumped in
with both feet. It wasn't the first time she'd turned to Ja
nette Cooper with a problem. Because Janette worked as a
clerk at the grocery store and because Perry shopped there
daily, a friendship had sprung up between the women.

"I have a problem."

"No kidding."

Perry playfully punched Janette's arm. "Be nice. I'm here
for help, not sarcasm."

"I was being nice. You only come here when you have a
problem. So, what is it this time? Did you forget how to
drain the water out of the tub? Or do you need another
cooking lesson?"

Perry glanced at her friend. A light breeze raised Janette
Cooper's shoulder-length blond hair from her shoulders
but it was mischief that put the twinkle in her green eyes
"What? Is there some sort of law on the books that says a
woman is instinctively supposed to know how to cook and
clean?"

"No. But you have to admit, draining the tub is sort of
elementary."

"Yeah, well, this problem is nothing like the others. It's
more complicated than any other problem I've come to you
with."

"Love usually is."

"Excuse me?"

"I said love usually is. Complicated, that is."

Totally stunned by Janette's perceptiveness, Perry sim
ply stared at her. "How did you know?"

Janette shrugged. "Wise beyond my years?"

"And a smarty-pants, too."

"But a wise smarty-pants." Smiling sympathetically, Ja
nette turned away from Mitzie and the beagles and leaned

against the thick wooden posts of the fence. "You've been living with a man twenty-four hours a day for the past month. He's bright, attractive and a heck of a lot of fun. And you're no slouch yourself."

"Thanks."

"You're welcome. The way I see this, you're both young, attractive and unattached. So what's the problem?"

"The problem is that I'm living a lie."

"I'm just about positive Mike's figured that out already," Janette sensibly suggested. "Lord knows I figured it out even before the cooking lessons."

"I guess I'm not as good an actress as I'd thought."

"Perry, I'd tell you not to quit your day job, but obviously you already have. So, let's cut through the bull. Why don't you just tell me the whole story?"

Perry took a deep breath and launched into an explanation that made Janette's eyes bulge. "Good Lord!" was all Janette could say when Perry ran out of steam.

"Pitiful, isn't it?"

"No," Janette said, sounding confused and slightly disoriented. "To be frank, Perry, aside from the bit about Arthur Tyrone, I don't really see that you have a problem."

"Janette, I have absolutely no idea how Mike McGuire feels about me. When I first came here, he tripped all over himself to keep from looking at me, and then we made this stupid pact agreeing not to give in to chemistry. There are times when I catch him looking at me the way he used to look at me, but his expression will go back to normal so quickly, I sometimes think I imagined everything...."

"And before you tell him anything, you want to be sure of how he really feels about you?"

"I want him to love me for me, and until he really falls in love with me, I can't tell him. But if I don't tell him, he's really not falling in love with me, because being wealthy is part of who I am, becoming CEO of Omnipotence is another part of who I am. It hit me this morning that I'm a lot more than my personality, I come with baggage."

"We should all be so lucky as to have your baggage," Janette muttered, then she laughed, hooking her foot against the fence post as she stared out at the now bare trees of the forest behind her house.

They were quiet for several minutes, leaning against the thick round poles of the wooden fence, watching Mitzie run with the beagles, screaming with happiness. Finally, Janette said, "I think I understand where you're coming from. I mean, I think I understand what you're trying to tell me."

"That my life is a mess? Or that my life is totally and completely complicated?"

"Would it really hurt so much to keep who you are a secret? Wouldn't it make sense to let this relationship develop naturally before you spring your real identity on him?"

"No. I feel like a fake and a liar. Besides, it's not fair. Do you realize that if we fall in love and marry, he'd have to move to Boston? He'd have to become part of a social circle that boggles the mind. I can't keep my identity a secret from him and let him think he's falling in love with a runaway hospital administrator. It wouldn't be fair."

"Then there's no way out of this," Janette lamented, a pleading tone in her voice as she touched Perry's arm. "Because, I know Mike. If you tell him before he's got really deep feelings for you, he'll hold himself so much in reserve around you, he'll never develop those feelings."

"My thought exactly," Perry agreed, then moved to open the gate. "Come on, Mitzie, we gotta go home."

Touching her sleeve again, Janette stopped her. "What are you going to do?"

This time, Perry shrugged, taking a deep breath as she did so. "I don't know. Eventually, I have to go back to Boston, but I don't want to leave with everything so confused. Even though I haven't heard from Cora, which means Arthur must still be stuck in Argentina and Mike's business problems are temporarily solved, I can't just hop in my car and disappear. I'd spend half of my life wondering if I'd thrown away my one chance at happiness and the other half wondering if I hadn't just imagined that I'm falling in love because, let's face it, I don't have confirmation of anything. All I have are a couple of suspicions, based on what I *think* is happening."

Janette brightened considerably. "So, you know what you have to do? Before you say one word to Mike McGuire, you have to figure out what *you're* really feeling."

"No kidding."

"You have to figure out if you truly are falling in love with Mike, or if you think you're falling in love with him because he's part of this life-style that you seem to love so much. A life-style which, coincidentally, has taken you away from some pretty sticky problems. Perry, there's a real possibility here that you've simply fallen in love with the idea of falling in love."

Janette's explanation made a great deal of sense to Perry. So much sense that she was afraid to ask her to continue, yet she felt strangely compelled to do so. "And?"

"And there's a really simple way to sort it all out."

Glancing at her friend suspiciously, Perry asked, "Which is?"

"Go bowling with him."

The pure absurdity of it made Perry burst into unrestrained laughter. "I beg your pardon?"

"Oh, Perry, you're so naive. Don't you know that if you can still think kindly of a man while you're involved in any kind of sport, you love him? Because even women who desperately love their husbands will neither bowl with them nor golf with them. It's sort of an unwritten rule because men turn into competitive beasts while on the playing field.

"Besides," Janette chided. "You said you wanted the full experience of living here on the outskirts of Ebensburg, and instead you've sort of locked yourself away in that house. Heck, you don't even visit me as often as you could ... and I've yet to feel comfortable visiting you."

This took Perry so much by surprise that she had to think about it a minute before responding. "Really?"

"Sure. You're not getting the whole movie here. You've found a frame you like and that's where you're staying. You, my dear, have got to get out more."

Perry blew her breath out on a long sigh. "You're right. I mean, here I am—as Cora would say—fussing and fuming and fretting, when I've only been here a month and I haven't really done anything except what has to do with my job."

"Great! Then come bowling tonight. It's mixed league night. So, you and Mike will fit in as if you belong there and nobody but you and me will know what's going on."

"Yeah, right. How, exactly, do I inform Mike that he's going bowling tonight?"

"You say, 'Mike, we've joined a bowling league.'"

"I don't even know if he bowls."

"All men bowl. Don't you ever watch 'The Flintstones'?"

"'The Flint'—what?"

Laughing, Janette put her arm around Perry's shoulders. "Never mind. Just tell Mike I talked you into joining a mixed league and ask if he's agreeable. If he says yes, I'll see you guys tonight at eight. If he says no, well, what the heck, you tried."

"A what?"

"I believe Janette said it was a mixed league."

"You mean one of those leagues where men and women bowl together?"

"Yes. Yes. That's exactly it."

"Oh, Perry, this is not a good idea."

It was to her. After having an entire day to think about it, Perry was primed and ready. She had no idea what people did when they bowled, but she did know it was out of the house, away from the kids and a quick, easy opportunity to see if she and Mike McGuire really were falling in love or if they were only compatible in this house, on this level.

"Please."

"Oh, Perry, men are so much better as bowlers than women that it takes all the fun out of it."

"I beg your pardon?"

"Men are stronger than women, so they just naturally bowl better."

She had no idea if that was true or not, but it sounded so chauvinistic and snotty that she decided it had to be wrong. "How can you say that?"

"Because it's true."

"I just think you're afraid that a woman might beat you and you can't handle that."

"Baloney."

"Prove it."

"All right, Miss High-and-Mighty, I will prove it. We'll join Janette's league."

So they called a baby-sitter, an eighteen-year-old named Melody with whom both the boys immediately became smitten and Mitzie immediately disliked.

"I don't want you to go!" she whined, hanging on to Perry's leg.

Mike unwrapped his daughter's fingers. "Mitzie, don't you think it's about time you gave Perry twenty minutes of peace and quiet?"

"No!" she wailed and threw herself around Perry's ankle.

"Come on, Mitzie," Melody chimed in. "I know how to make no-bake cookies."

That stopped her. "What're no-bake cookies?"

"Something like fudge but better because they have oatmeal in them."

Mitzie's blue eyes grew huge and luminescent. "Oatmeal?"

"Yeah. They're really good."

"Okay."

With that, she was off. Into the kitchen without a good-bye, leaving Perry standing disillusioned by the front door.

"It's a very odd feeling to be replaced by a cookie. Particularly a cookie that doesn't even have to be baked."

"Get used to it," Mike said and opened the door. "You'll be thrown over for stupider things than a cookie."

A thunderous crack greeted them as Mike opened the door to the bowling alley. The crack was followed by another, and then another and then another. Perry flinched and jumped so much, she was beginning to feel as if she had a nervous disorder.

"What size shoes do you wear?" Mike shouted to her as they approached a counter.

"Seven," she yelled, trying to be heard above the din. "Why?"

"So we can rent your bowling shoes," Mike answered sarcastically, throwing the statement back at her as if he thought she'd been sarcastic with him.

Perry's eyes widened in horror just as Janette sidled up next to her. "Don't say it," she warned in a whisper. "If you voice one word of protest about sticking your feet into a pair of shoes worn by no less than a thousand women, Mike will know something's up."

"You're such a comfort," Perry whispered back.

"I try."

"Here you go," Mike announced, approaching them from the counter. She had to admit he looked really good, and seeing him, the man in the tight jeans, the man with the beautiful black hair and gorgeous blue eyes, not to mention the knit shirt that proudly proclaimed, League Champs Six Consecutive Years, knowing that she was about to spend an evening with that man as her partner, made sticking her foot into a used shoe bearable. It also made her realize she was a lot more serious about their relationship than she'd thought. No wonder Janette had suggested bowling.

Even so, when he handed her the shoes, she got goose bumps. "Here you are, size seven. You put these on while I find a bowling ball I think you can handle."

"No, you go ahead," Janette said, waving him on with a quick motion of her hand. "Perry and I will find her ball."

The very second Perry thought Mike was out of earshot, she turned on Janette. "Are you sure this is hygienic?" she said, thrusting the worn and dirty shoes at her friend.

"What?" Janette innocently questioned. "Come on. We all wear socks and you can't get any life-threatening diseases from them. Be a sport."

A crash of thunder split the air and Perry jumped again. "Oh, I am so glad I listen to you."

"You will be after the night's over," Janette predicted authoritatively. "Look around, Perry Pierson. If you can love a man in this environment, you can love him anywhere."

Experiencing a spasmodic shiver as a result of another roar from exploding bowling pins, Perry had to admit her friend was probably correct.

"All right," Janette said, seizing Perry's arm and dragging her in the direction of a wall of brightly colored balls. "This will probably be the simplest thing you've faked since you got here. The object," she continued, pointing Perry to face the long shiny lanes, "is to throw a ball at those strange-looking wooden pegs called pins. Your goal is to knock all of them down the first time you throw the ball.''

"And if I don't?"

"You get a second chance, and if you make that, it's almost as good. Not quite, but almost." Janette reached out and took a bright pink ball from the wall. She handed it to Perry. "Don't worry about keeping score. Someone from your team will be designated to do that. All you have to do is remember your turn, throw the ball twice and smile a lot.''

The way Janette gave those instructions sent a shiver of fear down Perry's spine. "Why are you telling me all this?''

Janette drew a deep breath. "Because we didn't get lucky enough to get on the same team.''

Perry's eyes grew large with horror. "You mean I'm on my own?''

"Yes.''

"Oh, great!''

"Come on," Janette chided, tossing her arm across Perry's shoulders to lead her to her lane. "You can do it. Just watch what everybody else does.''

Far too quickly, Janette was gone. As Perry slid her feet into the well-worn red and green bowling shoes, she noticed Janette hadn't just been assigned to another team, she'd been assigned to the other side of the bowling alley. Perry closed her eyes and took a deep breath. Oh, well. What did she care? She wasn't here to win a trophy. She was here to see herself and the man wearing the League Champs Six Consecutive Years shirt in another environment. She glanced around at the long, shiny lanes. The bragging men. The chattering women. This certainly was another environment.

"Take your practice shot, Perry," Mike called out from his seat at the little table that sat at the foot of two lanes. Also behind the lanes but encircling the little table, the same way her sofa encircled the coffee table in front of the fireplace in her bedroom in Boston, was a blue and white plastic bench. From his location in the center of things, Perry assumed Mike was either their team captain, or scorekeeper, both of which seemed to be honored positions.

"Okay," she said and picked up the bright pink ball that she'd set beside her on the plastic seat. Watching other bowlers who were in various stages of their shot, Perry realized the object was to walk up to a dotted line, pause, pull the ball back and whale it at the pins, which might as well have been nine thousand miles away.

Feeling as if all eyes were on her, Perry walked to the dotted line, pulled her ball about halfway back, turned her head and looked at Mike. He encouraged her with a rolling motion of his hand. She nodded, smiled, faced the pins again and flung her arm back with a force so strong, she lost her grip on her ball and it flew backward before she could propel it forward. At least three people screamed and Perry spun around just in time to see everyone behind her duck.

Too stunned to move or speak, Perry stood helplessly while those who'd seen her faux pas laughed heartily and those who hadn't continued bowling. Mike scrambled from his seat, checked for injuries, grabbed her ball and joined her at the dotted line. "A little less force on the pull-back, okay?"

Red to the roots of her hair, Perry nodded. Mike backed away, Perry drew the ball back, and it seemed the entire room drew in a long anticipatory breath. But even before she could bring the ball forward, Mike yelled, "Stop!"

This time, Perry became irritated. "What?" she asked, spinning to face him.

"Perry, you have to start away from the line, so you can take a few steps forward before you throw the ball. Those few steps give you strength, momentum."

"So, what're you, an expert?"

He pointed to the writing on his left shirt pocket. League Champs Six Consecutive Years. Perry sighed. There really was no arguing with success.

Without turning around, she took six steps backward. Again, as she did so, she watched the other bowlers. They moved with an unusual grace and their movements were fluid. In fact, in a very real way, they reminded her of the girls in her ballet classes. Long fluid movements. Graceful steps. Fluid movements. Graceful steps.

Yeah. She could do this.

Thinking ballet, not bowling, Perry glided up to the dotted line. She didn't look at it or for it, just sensed the distance as she would when dancing with a partner. As she made the last two steps to the line, she pulled her arm back, thinking of herself as a graceful dancer at the Met, not a new bowler in Ebensburg. With all the ease and ability inspired by thousands of dollars of dancing lessons, Perry let go of her ball and watched it spin down the alley, crash into the pins and cause them to explode hard enough that those not knocked down by the ball were unbalanced by their neighbors until every pin landed on its side or off the alley.

There was a long, stupefied moment of silence, then groans of complaint by the people seated to Mike's left and shouts of joy from the people to Mike's right.

"Welcome aboard, kid," a fat man, smoking an even fatter cigar, told her as he wrapped his meaty arm around her slim shoulders. "What'd you say your friend's name was, Mike?"

He cleared his throat. "Perry."

"Well, Perry, I'm Ed. Ed Burnside. Damned glad you decided to join our league."

"Yeah, me, too," Perry agreed, turning to face Mike with a smile.

He scowled at her before looking down at the score sheet. "Nice move out there. Pretend you don't know how to bowl to give us a false sense of self-confidence, then get a strike. Funny, Perry. Really funny."

His chiding remarks confused Perry. "I thought you'd be glad I could bowl."

"No matter how much I like them, I'm never happy that the members of the opposing team can bowl like aces."

"You mean we're not on the same team?"

"Husbands and wives never are."

"But we're not married."

He sighed. "Nonetheless, we're a couple. So we're on different teams."

Stupid as it sounded, the thought pleased her. Not that she was on a different team, but that she was considered half of a couple. And when she realized the thought pleased her, her heart seemed to stop and sink simultaneously. Could she really have fallen in love with the idea of falling in love as Janette had suggested?

Seven frames into their game, the crowd had ground to an almost silent halt, and every time Perry rose to bowl, all eyes turned toward her. The first couple of strikes were called beginner's luck. They raised the hackles of the opposing players and had Mike close to furious. But when his teammates became disgusted, then angry, then furious, a strange thing happened. Mike first became calm and consoling, then he got angry, not with Perry but for Perry. If she got another strike and another bowler said the wrong thing, Perry feared a fight would break out.

The crowd broke into a deafening roar with her next strike. Applause rang out behind her. Only the people on the opposing team, Mike's team, remained still and silent. She waded through the congratulatory hugs and handshakes of people expecting her to bowl a perfect game and nervously took her seat on the thick plastic bench. Again, the crowd dispersed and returned to their normal games and Mike rose to take his turn.

Bringing his ball back, he walked forward, and when Rich Capretti thought Mike was out of earshot, he leaned into Perry's face and mumbled, "Ringer."

Perry didn't have time to register a reaction. As quickly as the word was spoken, Mike was beside her, hauling Rich off the plastic bench. "Apologize," he breathed in a voice so ominously quiet, it could make a mercenary flinch.

Rich's jaw was set in as firm a line as Perry had ever seen; his eyes were beady slits. Rather than apologize, he snapped, "What in the hell did you bring her for?"

"Because she's my friend. Because she needed a night out just like the rest of us."

"But, Mike, she's a damned ringer."

"I don't care if she's the chairman of the Republican National Committee. Everybody's welcome to bowl in this league, and even if they weren't, your behavior isn't representative of how my team behaves."

Perry felt a strange, rather unruly surge that combined an odd sense of fear and wonder. She wasn't afraid of Rich. Heck, she'd taken care of herself in worse situations. The absolutely unbelievable truth was, she didn't just love the man who had Rich Capretti by the shirt collar. He loved her too.

Or at least he loved a reasonable facsimile of Perry Pierson. He loved a housekeeper. He loved his daughter's baby sitter. He didn't love a billion-dollar heiress. And that's who she really was.

The ruckus quieted rather quickly. Apparently, disputes of this nature weren't abnormal and though everyone paused long enough to see who was disagreeing, no one ventured over, no one joined in. After a mumbled apology from Rich, no one would have known a fight had nearly started.

Perry got a spare, not a strike, on her next frame and even though her score was high—the highest recorded all night—

it wasn't perfect. The entire crowd thought the pressure and excitement of the night had taken its toll, but Perry knew better. She had a decision to make.

Tonight.

They couldn't go on like this. It simply wasn't fair. Either she gathered her courage and told Mike who she was and then faced the ramifications of that disclosure, or she left. It was that simple. If she left, she'd absolutely, positively lose Mike. If she told him the truth, there was about a ninety-percent chance she'd lose him. But at least she'd do it honestly.

Halfway through the third and final game, they were joined by a friend of Mike's, his co-worker, the man named Sam who'd told Perry he was Mike's best friend when she'd ventured into Mike's office with Mitzie on her first day of employment. While the other men had slapped her shoulder companionably, probably leaving her with a bruised back and offered their comments and criticisms on her game, this man smiled shyly and looked at the toe of his bowling shoe a lot.

"Tough break about your game."

Preoccupied with the weight of her decision, Perry had difficulty mustering an attention span. She forced herself to be more than polite, to be genuine and sincere to this friend of the man she'd want to grow old with if she didn't stand to inherit billions of dollars and more companies than any person could manage alone.

Glancing up at Sam, Perry smiled. "I thought I did very well." She lowered her voice conspiratorially. "Especially considering that this was my first game."

"Don't even try to feed us that line, Perry," Mike called over his shoulder as he prepared to make his shot. "We didn't buy it before. We don't buy it now."

Sam studied her for a full thirty seconds, then smiled. From the way his expression changed as he watched her,

Perry knew he was in some way, shape or form trained to deal with people, to read people and to judge people. "You're not lying, are you?"

Even if she wouldn't have realized she couldn't fool this man, Perry would have been honest with him. "No. This is my first game."

"Beginner's luck?" he asked, his eyes twinkling with laughter.

"Ten years of ballet lessons."

He was laughing heartily when Mike joined them and took the seat beside Perry on the plastic bench, because Sam had taken the scorekeeper's seat. "I have a favor to ask of you, Sam, since you guys got to bowl out tonight," Mike said, referring to the fact that Sam's competing team hadn't shown up, which meant Sam and his teammates would bowl normally and the other team would bowl some time during the week. Their scores would be compared to seek a winner. Having only half as many people playing meant they'd finished more quickly than the other bowlers and Sam was obviously socializing. "How about keeping our score, so I can concentrate on my game?" Mike said this as he put his arm across the back of the bench, behind Perry and sort of drew her closer to him. It was everything she could do to keep herself from nestling into his warmth.

Considering that this was neither the time nor the place, Perry contented herself with being close to him, with enjoying the simple pleasure of an absolutely normal, healthy, public display of affection. Maybe she could tell him? Maybe it wouldn't matter to him? Maybe he wouldn't mind being married to a socialite executive? Maybe he'd even like Boston?

Things were definitely looking up.

Smiling at Perry in a very flattering way, Sam said, "I'll be glad to sit here for the rest of the night and keep your score."

Two bowlers took their places on the lanes. Mike absently rubbed his fingers along Perry's shoulder and, still speaking with Sam, said, "By the way, after you left this afternoon, I got a special delivery."

Sam's hand stopped in place and he glanced over at Mike. "You're kidding?"

"Nope," Mike said and as he spoke the following words, the whole alley seemed to get absolutely quiet. "Only this one was different. This time, Omnipotence didn't just offer me a job, they offered to buy my paper. I don't know if they'll think I'm kidding or if they'll think I'm crazy, but I didn't find it complimentary that they want to put my paper in the hands of a junior executive as a training ground. And there's no way in hell I want to move to Boston to become a part of their corporate office. I don't want to be come out-of-touch executive. I want my hands on the paper, not a balance sheet. And I don't want to move. Not to Boston or anywhere else, for that matter. I wouldn't raise my kids anywhere but Ebensburg."

Perry froze. For what felt like minutes, her heart and lungs and muscles simply refused to function. Mike and Sam continued talking, discussing the offer with humor, while Perry simply breathed, reminding herself that if she registered any kind of reaction, if she burst into tears as she wanted to do, most of the adult population of the town would wonder why. Then she wouldn't merely blow her own cover, she'd expose Mike's problem. A problem he'd told her many times he took great pains to protect.

She finished the game in a numb state, said goodbye to Janette with real tears on the brims of her eyelids, then nestled into her seat in the car on the way home, pretending to be too tired to have a conversation.

She was going home.

To her real home.

In Boston.

Probably tonight.

No sense in prolonging the agony.

Chapter Fourteen

It was easier to get a flight out of Ebensburg than to compose her note of goodbye. She knew that was because she need only make one phone call to her father's pilot to get a plane. But she didn't know how to compose a note of goodbye. Worse, she didn't want to do it.

But she didn't have a choice. If there was one thing Cora had taught her, it was to be fair. And even though she wanted to stay here indefinitely, have the love of a wonderful man and be a mother to three terrific children, Perry knew it wasn't possible. She had responsibilities. She *had* to live in Boston. And, Mike, good father and generous man that he was, had his responsibilities, too. Only his were in Ebensburg. Nine hundred miles away from hers.

Nobody was right and nobody was wrong. But the truth of the matter was, their lives really and truly did not mesh. Spending the time to prove that would only hurt everyone more than leaving immediately would.

With a deep breath, Perry slid her pen from her stationery folder and pulled out one sheet of expensive bond. She cleared her throat, dabbed at the tears in her eyes and began writing. If he discovered she not only worked for Omnipotence but would someday own it, he might think she'd come here to spy, or, worse, to help Arthur. All she would allow herself to write was a brief explanation that she was leaving, a short paragraph stating how much she appreciated the time she'd spent with him and his family, a line about remembering them always and a thank-you.

After folding the note, she slid it into a matching envelope and propped it beside her lamp. Even as she pulled her hand away, her bedroom door creaked and Mitzie walked in, scraggly bear in her teeth and chocolate stains on the front of her thick flannel pajamas.

Ten shuffling steps had her across the room and attached to Perry's leg. "Mel-nee wouldn't let me wait for you."

Perry resisted the urge to bend down and scoop Mitzie into her arms. Instead, she cleared her throat, lowered herself to the bench seat by the vanity and turned to face Mitzie, woman to woman.

"Because your father and I didn't get home until after midnight and Melody knew little girls need their sleep."

Mitzie gave Perry a confused, pinched look, then said, "Are you crying?"

"Only a little," Perry admitted, but her voice quivered a lot.

Mitzie peered up at her, looking, it seemed, under the face Perry was trying to hide. "Why?"

"Because I'm just a little bit sad." Perry took a deep breath and reached out for Mitzie, settled her into her arms, then rose from her seat. "You've got to go back to bed."

Mitzie looped her arms around Perry's neck. "Let me sleep with you tonight."

"Can't."

"Please."

Perry smiled through her tears. "You're a conniver, Mitzie McGuire. But I've been around you long enough now that I know exactly what you're trying to do. And you're not going to get away with it. I'm putting you to bed."

It took another minute to convince Mitzie that she should go to her own room and another five minutes to settle her in bed. The close call hadn't just tugged on Perry's heartstrings, it had also shown her that she couldn't peek in on the sleeping twins, couldn't touch Mike's jacket or breathe in the scent of his briefcase. She had to go, or get caught leaving. Neither of which was a very happy prospect.

When Mike awakened the next morning, he went about his day, business as usual. Except he was humming. He hadn't expected to have fun the night before, and the excursion out had proved to him that he'd sheltered himself for too long. It was time to start his life again. Smiling as he jogged down the back stairs, Mike felt the weight of a million worries slip away. He felt the weight of years of pain disappear. He was over it. He was really and truly over the fact that his first marriage hadn't worked out.

And that really was the problem. His marriage had not worked out. There was no one to blame and no one at fault. He and Elaine simply were not compatible. True, she was a bit of a lowlife for deserting her children. But that had been for the best because Mike would have died if she'd taken his children with her when she left.

Despite three years of struggle and hiding behind work, everything had turned out for the best. Life was back to being good again, and Mike felt like a man who could do anything.

Seeing the kitchen light from the top of the steps didn't surprise him, but when he reached the kitchen and saw Mitzie standing on a chair in front of the cupboards, drop-

ping white bread into the toaster, he raced over to grab he
before she lost her balance and fell.

"Where's Perry?"

"She left."

The simple word really didn't sink in. "Left?"

"She was crying."

"Crying?" he asked, confused to the point that he wasn'
putting two and two together. He assumed that Perry ha
left the kitchen, but why she'd be crying, he had no idea
The only thing he did know was that it gave him a very od
feeling in the pit of his stomach.

Realizing that getting information from a confused four
year-old was fruitless, Mike set her on the floor, then piv
oted and raced up the stairs again. His heart absolutel
pounded in his chest. Sweat beaded on his forehead. Eu
phoria had been replaced by sickening fear. What if she ha
left? Really left. As in gone back home.

But why?

And why would she be crying?

Hope, more than anything else, forced him to knock o
Perry's bedroom door. Even when she didn't answer, h
knocked again, and again and again. Finally, inhaling
deep, courage-filled breath, Mike opened the door. In
stantly, his gaze caught the note, and in that simple space o
time, all the happiness he'd felt only minutes before evap
orated. That second made Elaine's screaming departur
seem like a happy day.

In fact, he felt feelings he didn't know a man could feel
Strong, compelling, masculine drives. The urge to scream
to pound something, was so strong, he almost couldn'
control it. Dammit! He'd happily, easily let Elaine out of hi
life. Were it not for the children, he wouldn't have notice
she was gone. And he couldn't understand why this strang
woman, this woman he'd known only a month, had brough
him to his knees with three short sentences.

He read her note again, and his heart sank. He had absolutely no idea where she was or, really, who she was. He sat on the bed. He'd lived so much in the present, he'd forgotten that sometimes the past holds some important keys.

Perry stepped out of the jet, accepting Jim's assisting hand. Her silk suit wasn't appropriate for the cool morning, so she walked quickly to the waiting limo. Someone would get her bags. Someone would retrieve the shiny blue ski jacket, rumpled jeans and blue T-shirt out of which she'd changed in the privacy of the plane's office cabin. Someone would be sent to retrieve her Audi from the small airport in Pennsylvania. Someone would drive her home. And no one would ask her about the sunglasses she wore in the predawn darkness.

She stepped into the limo, slid across the seat, and, without a word, closed her eyes. The kids would grow up and move on. So, in a sense, she'd faced the fact that she'd lose them eventually. But what she felt for Mike was different. She'd left half of herself nine hundred miles behind her. There'd never be another man with whom she could be so honest. There'd probably never be another man she'd love as easily or as openly.

There'd probably never be another man.

"Are you working today?"

"No. Why?"

"Then get your bottom to my office. In twenty, no, make it fifteen minutes. Perry's gone."

Janette Cooper gasped. "What? Why?"

Mike said, "I don't know. That's why I want to talk with you. My office. Fifteen minutes." He slammed the phone's receiver into its cradle and sincerely hoped Janette wouldn't disappoint him because in another hour or two, all this misery would sink in and he suspected he'd experience feelings the likes of which he'd never known before. He'd kept himself together to get the boys on the bus and Mitzie dressed and fed, but when this blessed numbness wore off, crumbling wasn't far behind. And when he crumbled, when he crawled into his ball of misery, he at least wanted to know why. Seeing the easy, genuine friendship that existed between Perry and Janette last night at the bowling alley, Mike had a sneaking suspicion Janette knew a lot more about this situation than he did.

Sam was opening the front door of the paper's office when Mike arrived. "Hey, you're here mighty early. You either couldn't control yourself at breakfast again, or you're trying to get enough work done that you can sneak home early." He watched as Mike reached into his car and pulled sleeping Mitzie into his arms and Sam's bright, happy mood quickly evaporated. "What's up?"

"Perry's gone," Mike woodenly reported, entering the quiet building behind his best friend.

"Gone?"

"She left. Her note didn't say where or why, but Janette Cooper's on her way. If anybody knows, Janette would know."

Sam scratched his head. "Holy cow."

Mike checked his watch and decided against calling his mother and asking her to come and get Mitzie. As long as Mitzie was sleeping, she wasn't a problem, and he wasn't quite ready to face his mother's I-told-you-so's yet. As he thought the last, he heard the squeal of tires in the gravel of his parking lot. Sam jumped up and looked out the window. "It's Janette Cooper."

Mike began walking toward his office. "Send her in."

* * *

Cora greeted Perry at the door. "Perry!"

Perry accepted her hug with a small smile and then backed away. "Good morning."

"Good morning my foot," Cora chided. "You don't call in the middle of the night, demand—yes, demand, young lady, your father will hear about this—that the jet travel nine hundred miles to an unknown airport in some godforsaken wilderness and then waltz in here and say good morning."

Perry uncharacteristically ignored her. "Where's Daddy?"

"He stayed in the city last night but he'll be home some time early this afternoon. Why?"

"No reason. I'm going up to my rooms and take a long slow bath. Would you mind having Mrs. Baker bring me a peanut butter and jelly sandwich and a glass of hot cocoa?"

Cora said nothing as she watched Perry glide up the circular stairway. But as soon as Perry was on the landing, Cora turned toward the kitchen and mouthed, "Peanut butter and jelly?"

Lord, things were worse than she'd thought.

Sam arrived in Mike's office toting a pot of piping hot coffee. "Thought you guys could use this."

"Thanks, Sam," Mike said, and when he noticed Sam wasn't leaving, but rather awkwardly standing by Mike's desk, he motioned toward the second chair. "You might as well sit, maybe you can help us figure this out. Janette and I are getting nowhere."

"She was a little confused," Janette said, herself sounding confused and slightly disoriented. "Well, maybe she was a lot confused. But we had a game plan and it was working and she was happy."

Mike shook his head. Sam frowned.

"In fact, the last time we talked, I got the impression that this was the first time in her life she'd ever really been happy."

"Maybe she couldn't deal with it. Or didn't know how to deal with it," Sam offered as he accepted a cup of coffee, which Mike was pouring.

"No," Janette insisted. "She was too tough. She jumped into some things I never thought she'd try and she handled them beautifully. She wasn't afraid of anything. You guys don't know the half of it."

"Then tell us," Mike offered reasonably.

The rest of the staff began to arrive and the noise of car engines, car doors and grumbled good mornings mixed with Mitzie's little moans and groans from her rolled-up position on the couch in Mike's office. Janette glanced first at Mike, then at Sam. "She never really swore me to secrecy, but some things you just know are secrets. It's like an instinct. I... I... can't tell you."

Mike swore ripely under his breath. Sam fell back on his seat.

"What do you mean, you can't tell me!" Mike demanded. "Is she a criminal?"

"No, she's not a criminal," Janette quietly said, her head bowed.

There was a moment of silence, a long moment of silence in which one could hear a clock tick, and suddenly the newsroom erupted with noise and confusion and within seconds Mike's mother burst into his office, unannounced and panting from exertion.

"She's an heiress!" Mary McGuire cried, entering the room as if floating on a cloud. "An heiress! Her father is Graham Pierson."

Sam's eyes grew to twice their size and he whistled with respect. Mike's eyes closed and he groaned with frustration.

"What are you doing here, Mother?"

Mary took a deep breath. "Well, after our conversation last month, I suspected you weren't going to do anything to check out the woman who was taking care of my grandkids. I waited a week, actually I waited two for you to do something, then I took matters into my own hands."

Janette and Sam snickered and looked away. Mike exhaled a long exasperated breath.

"And *I* hired the investigator. And at six o'clock last night, he gave me this," she said, reaching into a huge denim tote to retrieve a thin manila file, which she handed to Mike. "I tried to call you last night, but you weren't home. I tried to call this morning, but obviously you'd already gone. So, here I am."

Almost against his better judgment, Mike reached out and took the folder.

"There's really not much on her personal life." Mary laughed. "It's almost as if she doesn't have one. But look at those charities. My God, she's chaired everything from the American Cancer Society to Friends of Furry Friends. And her address," Mary added, rounding the desk to point it out to her son, "is right here. This is her real address and phone number. I called the number last night and they answered the phone by saying Pierson Estates."

"Mother, I can't believe you did this. It's an absolutely disgusting invasion of privacy." He turned to Janette. "I guess this is what you know that the rest of us didn't."

Janette nodded solemnly.

Mike took a long breath. "Well, now I have all the information I need, except the most important piece. If I don't know why she left, I don't know if I can convince her to come back."

"Of course, you'll convince her to come back," Ma insisted, her eyes wide with horror at the thought that might not. "You can't let a woman like this get away."

"Mother," Mike said exasperatedly, "she is nothing, absolutely nothing like you think! You may not want her for a daughter-in-law...."

"Besides," Janette chided, "if Perry marries Mik chances are they wouldn't stay here—couldn't stay her She's already running Pierson Publications, but she's only child, so the burden of running her father's enti conglomerate will one day fall to her and only her. They not only be forced to move to Boston, but they'd spend much time in the executive suite, you'd never see the again...."

Blinking rapidly, Sam rose. "Oh, my God."

"What?" Mike demanded. "What?"

"Pierson Publications. That's part of Omnipotence."

As the full implication of that statement sunk in for Mi and Sam, Janette and Mary sat staring at both of them e pectantly. Mitzie chose that precise moment to awaken a shuffle over to her father. She walked behind his desk, rais herself to his lap and snuggled into his neck.

Stroking Mitzie's back, Mike said, "I think that sort answers everything." Then he rose from his seat. "Mothe would you mind caring for Mitzie today?"

"Of course, dear," Mary replied, taking the sleepy M zie from his arms.

"Good. Janette, thank you for coming."

"You're welcome, I guess," Janette replied, slowly r ing from her seat.

Mike waited until his mother and Janette had exited h office, then he turned to his friend. "I guess you can g back to work now."

Sam cleared his throat. "Don't you want—"

"To talk about this? I don't think so. Give me a few days of feeling foolish privately before I have to go public with the fact that I not only let a spy from Omnipotence move in, I kissed her. I helped her. I aided and abetted my own enemy."

Chapter Fifteen

Mike stayed stunned for only an hour, then he got angr
Really angry. But given that the whole world would soo
know he'd been duped, Mike wasn't surprised. Still, th
public aspect of his problem didn't stop him from wantir
a confrontation, it merely caused him to be very caref
about how he got out of town.

He called Janette and asked her to watch the kids for
few days, explaining that he needed some time alone, an
she tearfully complied. He gave Sam full control over th
paper for the next week, and Sam solemnly nodded.

With those two tasks completed, Mike turned to h
mother who had returned to his office with breakfast in
picnic basket. "I'm not going to say I'm not glad you ha
Perry investigated," he admitted quietly. "But if you eve
do anything even remotely close to interfering in my li
again, I'm not going to be so polite."

"But, Mike—"

"I mean it, Mother. I'm thirty-six. I can take care of my-self. If you're bored," he added, tossing the manila folder at his mother, "why not take a cue from Perry and get in-volved someplace where you're not just needed, but appre-ciated—a good charity."

With that, he rounded his desk and walked out of his of-fice. In another two hours, he was in the air, on his way to Perry's house.

Cora didn't even have to ask who he was.

Black hair.

Blue eyes.

Sculptured chin.

And, probably, beneath that tweed jacket were the mus-cles of a guy who chopped wood.

She hadn't gotten much out of Perry that morning, ex-cept that their secret was safe. Mike didn't know who Perry was, and even if he had enough information to find her home because he knew her name, that still didn't mean he'd made the association between the Piersons and Omnipo-tence. At least Perry hoped not.

Cora heaved a sigh and pulled open the door. "Come in," she said, her tone of voice that of a woman resolved to the whims of fate. "I'll get her."

Cora turned to walk away but he stopped her. "But you don't—"

"Know who you are? Guess again. I don't even have to ask your name to know that you're Mike McGuire."

Her voice was noncommittal this time, and even though that had Mike wondering about the wisdom of his deci-sion, the fact that she agreed to go and get Perry lifted his spirits a bit. At least he didn't have to get past an army of butlers and secretaries as he'd feared in the airplane, and at least he didn't have to make an awkward explanation of who he was. And in another few minutes, he'd get the satisfaction—finally—of confronting someone from Omnipotence.

All the same, he wasn't prepared for the sight of Perry as she walked down the circular stairway. For the first time since the day she'd come to his home seeking employment, she wore makeup, not so much that she looked artificial, but just enough to enhance her natural beauty and to make her look as elegant as the home in which she lived.

If that alone wouldn't have been enough to make him stop in his tracks, her simple blue silk sheath would have done the trick. Either that or the diamond and pearl combs nestled in the sweep of her hair, which gracefully framed her face then rolled up and around into a sculptured chignon. Her appearance and demeanor was such a far cry from odd colored sweat suits, no jewelry and hair that bounced and bobbed as it pleased, that Mike stood stunned, speechless.

"Good afternoon," she greeted coolly, even as she descended the stairway.

When she reached the bottom step, she offered her hand, and Mike didn't know whether to take it or shake it—or shake her.

In the end, he lightly gripped her hand, kind of shook it, kind of squeezed it slightly and then let her pull it away.

"Please," she said, gesturing with a well-manicured right hand. "Join me for lunch. I'm afraid I don't have much time. I returned to a mountain of paperwork."

She didn't give him a chance to respond and instead began walking down a long hall. The richly paneled walls made the corridor so dark that all three of the brass and crystal light fixtures were needed to light it.

Mike looked around, dread and something akin to fear beginning to bubble in his veins. He understood perfectly well why Perry would have chosen to run away from this. She didn't have a life. She appeared to be in a very fancy, very quiet prison.

Either Perry typically dined with someone, or she'd gotten word to the staff to set another place because the instant they arrived in the huge formal dining room, a short chubby maid pulled away from arranging a second place setting at the table and darted behind a door. Perry gestured toward one of the two place settings and proceeded to seat herself at the other.

Quickly coming out of his state of shock, if only temporarily, Mike jumped to help her with her chair. She smiled and nodded her approval and politely waited for Mike to be seated before she asked if he'd like coffee.

"Yes," he said, expecting Perry to reach for the silver coffee service, which was set off to her left. Instead, she rang a bell, the short maid appeared, and, upon Perry's instructions, the woman poured the coffee.

"My God, Perry," Mike said the minute the door closed behind the servant. "How can you live like this?"

"I don't understand what you're talking about."

"This," he said, sweeping his arm around in a gesture that took in more than the entire room, more than the house, more than the grounds, more than Boston. The gesture seemed to indicate a way of life.

She sighed and then surprised him by refilling her own coffee cup after nervously drinking the first one. When she spoke, her voice and tone were the one he remembered. "You get used to it."

Relaxing, Mike glanced around again. "Somehow I doubt that."

"Oh, no. Really. You do," Perry insisted, peeking at him over the coffee cup.

Her doelike brown eyes would always melt his heart, they told him more than her words ever had. He'd miss that. Miss being so close to someone, so naturally close that they could communicate on more than one level. That made life simple, beautiful, special. Just like the woman beside him.

Regardless of the fact that she was born into all this, he couldn't reconcile himself to the fact that she actually liked it here.

Mike took a long breath, swallowed hard and said, "It's a nice place to visit, Perry."

"But you wouldn't want to live here?" she asked, then she started to laugh, lightly, airily, as if she didn't have a care in the world. "I already knew that."

Once again uncomfortable, Mike cleared his throat. "I'm sorry about the conversation you overheard last night. If I'd known—"

"Don't be," Perry interrupted before he could complete the thought, and Mike was glad because right now, in this room, he wasn't really sure how he would have completed it. "You trusted me enough to discuss a business matter in front of me and what I will remember of that episode wasn't the impact of what you said, but rather that you and Sam trusted me enough to say it."

"But you don't understand...."

"Of course, I do. My God, Mike, look around you. Do you want Mitzie to be raised here?"

Agreeing with her, he closed his eyes and answered honestly. "No."

"Neither do I."

Pushing her lunch away, Perry set her elbows on the table in front of her and balanced her chin on her entwined fingers. She didn't look at him but rather stared out the sheer curtain covering the huge window to her left. "So now that you've figured everything out, I gather you want me to apologize."

"No," he admitted quietly. "I came here to give you a good piece of my mind."

She smiled, opening her hands. "Feel free. I'm sure you think I deserve it."

"Why shouldn't I?" Mike thundered and rose from his chair to pace. He wasn't angry with her for duping him anymore, he was angry with her for playing this foolish game of hide-and-seek with him now. He didn't like this cool, calm, collected stranger Perry kept turning into and he suspected that was half the reason she did it. As long as she kept her distance, there'd be no danger that they'd actually talk about the real issues. "Damn it! Why shouldn't I?" he said again, and whirled to face her.

As he shouted, he watched her facade slip a bit, not into fear or sadness, but into a set of expressions and gestures he recognized—gestures he considered to be manifestations of her real personality—and he realized that if he wanted to talk with her, really talk with her, get the chance to get to the bottom of this mess, he'd have to push her to be honest with him, and it looked as if he was doing that by making her mad.

"How could you expect me not to be angry with you?" he added, ready to say the words he didn't really believe, but had once suspected, words that would probably send her into a fit of rage. "Now that I know who you are, everything falls into place. You didn't just appear at my house out of the blue, you'd planned to be there. I understand."

"You understand nothing!" His anger fueled hers and she rose from her chair. "And," she added, her tone matching his, her voice as loud as his, "if I remember correctly, you have no one to blame but yourself. Do you want to know why I was at your house that morning?"

"Oh, please," he said sarcastically. "I'm breathless with anticipation."

"Well, you sanctimonious twit! Even after I pointed out to you three times that you *left me* with Mitzie, you still refuse to take the blame for any of this." Even as she said the last, another thought struck her and she began to laugh.

"That's the real problem, isn't it? You're more to blame for this mix-up than I am and you're angry with yourself, not me."

"Huh! Fat chance!" he countered, pacing away from her. "Do you think I would have trusted Mitzie with you if you would have told me the truth? That you're a pampered heiress who's never even taken care of herself, let alone a child?"

"Who cares?" she snapped, following him and snagging his arm to spin him around. "The point is, you did and I didn't disappoint you. I came through for you and for your kids. And I didn't do it for myself."

"Baloney!"

"Baloney?" she gasped, righteous indignation compelling her to step closer, stand on tiptoe and face him head-on. "I'd come to your house, away from the prying eyes and ears of your employees, to offer to help you best Arthur Tyrone."

"Oh, that's a hot one, Perry. Because by the time you came around, Arthur had vanished. In fact, now that I think about it, you left Ebensburg the minute you discovered Arthur was back in the picture. So, what the hell was it you really wanted from me? And why me? What could you possibly want from me?"

"Nothing!" she shouted. "Absolutely nothing. Don't you see? By the time I was knee-deep in housework—your housework," she added pointedly, "I realized this wasn't your fight, but mine. I was there, at your house, because my father didn't trust me. I told you that. No matter how it looks, I was wrestling with issues that had nothing to do with you."

"Not true," he countered slowly. "You wanted something from me. Admit it, Perry. At least admit it to yourself."

"What in the hell do you think I could possibly think I'd even in my wildest dreams get from a reclusive divorcé who's so defensive that he can't even keep a housekeeper?"

"This," Mike easily replied, grabbing her upper arms with his hands and lifting her until he could seize her lips with his own. Instead of meeting the resistance he expected, he found Perry's mouth hot and hungry beneath his. He pulled her closer, devouring her mouth with his own, even as he wondered how the hell they were going to get themselves out of this mess. His tongue played at the corners of her mouth until, properly coaxed, she opened her lips and her own tongue greeted his. They kissed hungrily, greedily for a full minute, both desperate, both lost.

Then a soft-spoken, cultured, yet somehow horrified tone carried the words, "Perry, my God, what are you doing?" into the room, and they sprung apart as guilty as teenagers.

Perry croaked, "Daddy?"

But Mike mumbled, "We have definitely got to do something about our parents."

Chapter Sixteen

"**D**addy! It's so good to see you!"

While Perry rounded the table and quickly made her way over to her father, Mike stared at Graham Pierson. There was something about him that just didn't sit right. Something about him, something confusing, something off balance, that gave Mike an odd, unsettling feeling. Perry kissed her father's cheek and Mike continued to stare.

Dressed like a well-heeled businessman, Graham Pierson wore an expensive black suit, equally expensive white shirt and a red tie that probably cost a week's salary. But Mike expected that or something similar.

Eyes roving cautiously, Mike continued to take inventory of Perry's father. His blond hair hadn't been styled, just properly cut, and straight yellow locks lay quite normally on the man's quite normal head. Graham Pierson's eyes were brown like his daughter's and his clean-shaven face, though handsome, was still about as average as a face could get.

Mike had absolutely no idea what he was expecting from Perry's father, but this wasn't it.

Coming out of his reverie, Mike heard Perry say, "Cora told me she hasn't explained anything to you about my recent—disappearance."

"No, she hasn't," Graham said quietly, drilling his daughter with a very fatherly stare of disapproval.

"Well," Perry said, then she cleared her throat. To Mike, it looked as if she was gathering her courage because she straightened her spine, turned and looked her father right in the eye. "This is Mike McGuire, Dad. Mike, this is my father. I went down to visit Mr. McGuire because Arthur has been taking over small newspapers like Mr. McGuire's by literally stealing their employees until the newspapers are so short-staffed, they can no longer produce a paper and they fold. When that happens, Arthur simply moves in, telling you he's found a new territory for one of our existing enterprises. Not only did I consider that out of character for the way Omnipotence does business, but I personally consider it unethical. I didn't come to you because I didn't think you'd believe me over Arthur, and what I'd hoped to do was gather enough evidence from Mr. McGuire that I could prove what Arthur was doing so you could handle the situation."

Perry's father listened attentively, but didn't say anything. Mike felt sweat beading on the back of his neck, and he couldn't stand the silence one second longer. "If it's proof you want," Mike piped in, "I can give you tons of it because Perry's theory is a hundred percent on the money. In fact, I think you should be damned proud of her. Not only was Perry trying to save Omnipotence's reputation, but she did a damned fine job as a housekeeper."

Graham cast a peculiar look in Mike's direction, and despite the fact that Mike could tell Perry's father tried to stop himself, his expression shifted from a cold stare into an amused look, and he faced his daughter again. "A house-keeper?" he said, blinking rapidly. *"You worked as a housekeeper?"*

Perry's spine stiffened again. "Omnipotence's reputation was on the line. And I knew you wouldn't listen to me."

"But a housekeeper?" he asked, his voice and expression betraying his confusion. "What does working as a housekeeper have to do with saving Omnipotence?"

"I went to solicit Mr. McGuire's help. He needed a housekeeper, and I took the job so I could be close enough that I could try to get information out of him, or if necessary, snoop."

"My God! This is unbelievable! How the devil did you ever convince this man to hire you?"

Perry cleared her throat. "Well, he didn't have a choice. I sort of took the job by default."

Then, Graham smiled with his entire face. His eyes lit, his mouth bowed, even his skin seemed to glow with approval. As if he'd thought the thing through and decided he could not only accept it, but appreciate it, he burst into laughter. "My God, man! How'd you survive? Perry's my daughter and I love her dearly, but I wouldn't let her make me a cup of tea."

Mike cleared his throat. "Actually, Perry was the best housekeeper we ever had."

Graham laughed with delight. "You must have been desperate!"

"Oh, we were," Mike agreed, though he knew he and Perry's father were probably talking about two different things. "Mitzie, my daughter," he explained, "blossomed under Perry's care. The twins actually read books. I had someone to talk with at the end of the day."

A lump the size of a tennis ball formed in Perry's throat. She'd never felt so needed in her whole life. Not because of Mitzie and the twins, but because of the wobbly note in

Mike's voice when he'd made the simple confession about having somebody to talk with at the end of the day. Had they been in a position to marry, they would have shared evenings with the kids and passionate nights with each other. Mike would have had someone to help with his life, to understand him, and someone upon whom to shower all that affection he'd welled up for so long that he looked like a man on the verge of exploding.

Graham, however, frowned. "Looks and sounds to me like we got beyond housekeeping."

Mike looked at Perry. Perry looked at Mike. By unspoken agreement, Perry responded to the backhanded question. "Yes and no. I mean, once we realized we'd fallen in love..."

She said the words so easily, so beautifully, that Mike looked over at her. She loved him. This sassy, spunky woman, with a heart of gold and nerves of steel loved him. He knew it, of course, he'd just never heard her say it.

"We... I decided that before Mitzie or the boys or even Mike got too attached to me, I'd better leave."

Looking confused, Graham sat on a nearby chair. For a full minute, he said nothing, then he sighed. "I don't believe I've taught you to run from love."

"Oh, you didn't," Perry hastened to assure her father. "It's just that Mike has responsibilities he can't leave. Plus, he has the children. And I have responsibilities here that I'm fully prepared to assume when the time comes. We might have loved each other...." She paused, looked at Mike and smiled in such a way that his heart broke. "We do love each other. But we live in two different worlds, and we're wise enough to accept that."

Graham glanced at Mike. "Then, why's he here? If you two are so wise that you can accept that you can't live in each other's worlds, why's he here now?" Perry opened her mouth to speak, but Graham rose. "No. Sorry, count me out on this. This, I believe, should be private. Besides, I think I've got to make a trip into the office. Arthur Tyrone has more than a little explaining to do." He turned, and, shaking Mike's hand, he added, "Mr. McGuire, it was my pleasure to meet you. Rest assured, Omnipotence will make full restitution for any damage caused by Mr. Tyrone's interference. As for the rest of this, the two of you are on your own."

Mike was so impressed by the fact that Perry's father not only took Perry's word about Arthur Tyrone without the proof Mike could have given, but by the fact that he left the room without interfering in Perry's personal life, that he stood, stunned, and merely stared at the exquisite wooden portal through which Graham Pierson had walked. Here was a man with more money and power than nearly everyone else on the face of the earth, and he was wise enough to stay out of his child's love life. Mike almost couldn't believe it, particularly when he considered the guy wasn't any different, or any older, and therefore, shouldn't be any wiser, than his own parents.

That was it! Graham Pierson was young! That was the odd thing about him that Mike couldn't put his finger on! Because Graham Pierson was so successful and so powerful, Mike had expected him to be much older. But more than that, the way Perry worried about taking over for him when he retired, Mike had assumed his retirement was just around the corner.

"Perry, how old's your dad?"

She glanced at him. "Fifty-six."

"Fifty-six," he shouted, grabbed her around the waist and jubilantly spun her around. "Even if your father retires at the normal age, sixty-five, that's nine years from now."

He stopped the spin and gave her a smacking kiss before he set her on her feet again. Confused, Perry stared at him. "So?"

"So, we could have nine very happy, very normal years in Ebensburg before we'd have to move here."

She blinked, comprehension coming to her slowly. "Well, sort of."

Cautiously, he backed away. "What do you mean, sort of?"

"Well, I do have certain things I do here. You know, one of the companies is fully under my control. I have a staff, so I don't have to be here all the time, and some of the things could even be handled by fax and modem, but I also have my charities. And there are holidays...."

"Yeah," he said, feeling himself deflate again.

She peeked up at him. "But if we figured out a way to divide the time and the responsibilities..."

He glanced at her. "You mean, if we compromised?"

"Yes. If we compromised somewhat, we wouldn't just have nine reasonably normal years, we could actually have a reasonably normal life. If we ran Omnipotence together, neither one of us would be overburdened."

Again the room became totally silent. It was, in reality, the moment of truth. Both took a deep breath. Both looked at their shoes. Both waited for the other to speak. Finally, Mike broke the silence.

"Wanna come back with me and see how it goes?"

Perry continued to look at her toes. "No."

"No?" Mike croaked, positive he must have misunderstood. "Perry, I'm damned certain we just got your father's blessing."

"I know."

"Then, what...why...?"

Boldly, she brought her gaze from the floor, took a deep breath of air and looked him right in the eye. "I'm not go-

ing to live with you. And I'm not going to subject Mitzie and
the twins to wondering every time we fight if I'll leave or
you'll kick me out. I think our children need a commitment. I want you to marry me.''

No one had ever proposed to Mike before. No one had
ever laid claim to his children—not even their real mother.
His throat closed and it became difficult to speak.

''Please don't think that stalling for time will change my
mind. I love you. I have no doubts,'' she said.

''I love you, too,'' Mike said, then seized her upper arms
and pulled her up for a soul-melting kiss.

*   *   *   *   *

Take 4 bestselling love stories FREE

Plus get a FREE surprise gift!

Special Limited-time Offer

Mail to Silhouette Reader Service™

3010 Walden Avenue
P.O. Box 1867
Buffalo, N.Y. 14269-1867

YES! Please send me 4 free Silhouette Romance™ novels and my free surprise gift. Then send me 6 brand-new novels every month, which I will receive months before they appear in bookstores. Bill me at the low price of $2.19 each plus 25¢ delivery and applicable sales tax, if any.* That's the complete price and—compared to the cover prices of $2.75 each—quite a bargain! I understand that accepting the books and gift places me under no obligation ever to buy any books. I can always return a shipment and cancel at any time. Even if I never buy another book from Silhouette, the 4 free books and the surprise gift are mine to keep forever.

215 BPA ANRP

Name	(PLEASE PRINT)	
Address	Apt. No.	
City	State	Zip

Beginning in August from Silhouette Romance...

WEDDING WAGER

by Sandra Steffen

Three sexy, single brothers bet they'll never say "I do." But the Harris boys are about to discover their vows of bachelorhood don't stand a chance against the forces of love!

Don't miss:

BACHELOR DADDY (8/94): Single father Mitch Harris gets more than just parenting lessons from his lovely neighbor, Raine McAlister.

BACHELOR AT THE WEDDING (11/94): He caught the garter, she caught the bouquet. And Kyle Harris is in for more than a brief encounter with single mom Clarissa Cohagan.

EXPECTANT BACHELOR (1/95): Taylor Harris gets the shock of his life when the stunning Gina Jenson asks him to father her child.

Find out how these confirmed bachelors finally take the marriage plunge. Don't miss WEDDING WAGER, only from

Silhouette
R O M A N C E™

It's our 1000th Silhouette Romance™, and we're celebrating!

And to say "THANK YOU" to our wonderful readers, we would like to send you a

FREE AUSTRIAN CRYSTAL BRACELET

This special bracelet truly captures the spirit of CELEBRATION 1000! and is a stunning complement to any outfit! And it can be yours FREE just for enjoying SILHOUETTE ROMANCE™.

FREE GIFT OFFER

To receive your free gift, complete the certificate according to directions. Be certain to enclose the required number of proofs-of-purchase. Requests must be received no later than August 31, 1994. Please allow 6 to 8 weeks for receipt of order. Offer good while quantities of gifts last. Offer good in U.S. and Canada only.

And that's not all! Readers can also enter our...

CELEBRATION 1000! SWEEPSTAKES

In honor of our 1000th SILHOUETTE ROMANCE™, we'd like to award $1000 to a lucky reader!

As an added value every time you send in a completed offer certificate with the correct amount of proofs-of-purchase, your name will automatically be entered in our CELEBRATION 1000! Sweepstakes. The sweepstakes features a grand prize of $1000. PLUS, 1000 runner-up prizes of a FREE SILHOUETTE ROMANCE™, autographed by one of CELEBRATION 1000!'s special featured authors will be awarded. These volumes are sure to be cherished for years to come, a true commemorative keepsake.

DON'T MISS YOUR OPPORTUNITY TO WIN! ENTER NOW!

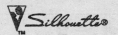

CELOFFER

CELEBRATION 1000! Free Gift Offer

ORDER INFORMATION:

To receive your free AUSTRIAN CRYSTAL BRACELET, send three original proof-of-purchase coupons from any SILHOUETTE ROMANCE™ title published in April through July 1994 with the Free Gift Certificate completed, plus $1.75 for postage and handling (check or money order—please do not send cash) payable to Silhouette Books CELEBRATION 1000! Offer. Hurry! Quantities are limited.

FREE GIFT CERTIFICATE   096 KBM

Name:_____

Address:_____

City:_____ State/Prov.:_____ Zip/Postal:_____

Mail this certificate, three proofs-of-purchase and check or money order to CELEBRATION 1000! Offer, Silhouette Books, 3010 Walden Avenue, P.O. Box 9057, Buffalo, NY 14269-9057 *or* P.O. Box 622, Fort Erie, Ontario L2A 5X3. Please allow 4-6 weeks for delivery. Offer expires August 31, 1994.

PLUS

Every time you submit a completed certificate with the correct number of proofs-of-purchase, you are automatically entered in our CELEBRATION 1000! SWEEPSTAKES to win the GRAND PRIZE of $1000 CASH! PLUS, 1000 runner-up prizes of a FREE Silhouette Romance™, autographed by one of CELEBRATION 1000!'s special featured authors, will be awarded. No purchase or obligation necessary to enter. See below for alternate means of entry and how to obtain complete sweepstakes rules.

CELEBRATION 1000! SWEEPSTAKES
NO PURCHASE OR OBLIGATION NECESSARY TO ENTER

You may enter the sweepstakes without taking advantage of the CELEBRATION 1000! FREE GIFT OFFER by hand-printing on a 3" x 5" card (mechanical reproductions are not acceptable) your name and address and mailing it to: CELEBRATION 1000! Sweepstakes, P.O. Box 9057, Buffalo, NY 14269-9057 *or* P.O. Box 622, Fort Erie, Ontario L2A 5X3. Limit: one entry per envelope. Entries must be sent via First Class mail and be received no later than August 31, 1994. No liability is assumed for lost, late or misdirected mail.

Sweepstakes is open to residents of the U.S. (except Puerto Rico) and Canada, 18 years of age or older. All federal, state, provincial, municipal and local laws apply. Offer void wherever prohibited by law. Odds of winning dependent on the number of entries received. For complete rules, send a self-addressed, stamped envelope to: CELEBRATION 1000! Rules, P.O. Box 4200, Blair, NE 68009.

 ONE PROOF OF PURCHASE

096KBM